The Lost
Firefly

Kayleigh Burdett

The Lost Firefly

DEDICATION

This is dedicated to my Grandad, Cyril Fox
My Hero, my mentor in life.

The Lost Firefly

CONTENTS

The Lost Firefly

ACKNOWLEDGMENTS

I would like to make it known, yes I was inspired by Alice in Wonderland,
Who wouldn't want to find a magical door, go within, make
Wonderful friends?

So thank you Mr Lewis for the wonderful inspirational world that is Alice in
wonderland, I'm sure your words will live on and inspire the next
generation.

The Lost Firefly

Chapter One

A Girl Called Raine

Raine was just like any other girl of 17, she took pride in her appearance, she went to school every day and she enjoyed her home life. Unfortunately she was also a loner at times, she did not like the company of people her own age. Then again she did not really like hanging out with any one in her small village and her family would never let her go out alone much.

Raine was very bright for her age, she enjoyed history and art lessons the most in school and was often picked on for her silent, lonely nature within school. Raine had never felt she fit in with any of the groups in the halls of her small village school. She could run, but did not fit in with the PE groups, she was smart, but not enough for the book clubs. She cared about her appearance but not enough to fit in with the more popular girls. In fact Raine was either ignored most of the day or teased in some form or another.

"It's strange to have two different colour eyes." They would say in the changing rooms.

"You're such a loner, look at her, sitting there like she doesn't hear us." The play grounds had always been a hard place to hide. Yet she found secondary school had larger places to hide and the break time taunts were less and less. It seemed to Raine if you had just one small thing different to the rest of the crowd you was shunned. Yet, this did not bother her now, when she was younger she would go home to her Aunties and cry to them, questioning why she had one green eye and one blue eye. They had always told her she was special, even the man who lived with them, Louie said she should never worry about what others thought about her eye colour, she should just ignore them.

Raine woke up one bright and sunny morning with a feeling today was going to be different, she smiled to herself as she choose her outfit for the day that it would be the same as always. Even as she sang in the shower she still tried to convince herself that today would be different, something would be different, no matter how small.

"Maybe I will win the lottery." She smiled walking down to the kitchen where the smell of coffee and toast drifted to her nose.

"Good morning dear, did you sleep well?" Auntie Maud smiled over the coffee pot and tended to something cooking on the stove. No doubt it would be pancakes, every Friday Auntie Maud would cook pancakes for breakfast and beef for dinner. Beef with potatoes from the garden and peas from her window box.

"Yes, very well Auntie thank you." Replied Raine sitting down in her normal spot by the window. She liked sitting by the window, she could see the hills rising in the distance.

"Here you are, a fresh glass of orange juice from the garden." Said Auntie Pearl with a bright smile.

"We have had a very good crop this year wouldn't you say ladies?" Asked Auntie Iris, the two women nodded their agreement and continued to busy themselves around the small kitchen of their cottage.

She was never sure if they were sisters or just related, Raine had never asked about her family much since she turned sixteen. On the night of her sixteenth birthday Auntie Pearl had sat with her in the garden. Auntie Pearl seemed to like the garden the most out of the whole house, she spent so much time there. She would laugh and say she must have been born in a garden, that she had earth running through her body and that was why she had green eyes.

One that particular night all three Aunties and Louie had made a fuss of her, they had showered her with gifts and everything she could have possibly wanted. Everything except answers. Yet, as Auntie Pearl spoke to her she finally told her about her parents, she told her that there was a war in her home land and the four of them were asked to take here away until it was over. Raine and many other children had been taken from their homes and taken to the countryside. It was unfortunate that Raine's parents was one of the many that did not come and collect their baby, so Auntie Maud, Iris, Pearl and Louie became her guardians.

"Louie, there you are, I was beginning to wonder where you were." Louie was such a lovely man with his floppy, brown hair and sea blue eyes with thick rimmed glasses. Raine smiled as he sat down beside her rather sadly. "What's wrong Louie, you look so sad this morning."

"It's nothing you can help with I'm afraid Raine, but thank you for asking." He reapplied with such a sad tone that Raine placed her hand on his shoulder and gave it a little squeeze. She hated to see Louie so unhappy, but he said there was nothing she would do, maybe she would make him a nice cake after school.

"I'm off to school today, not a children's school you know, grown up school."

"I know Raine," he sighed, that normally started off their game of 'What I do,' a game they used the play in order to make Raine have a better memory.

"Breakfast!" Called Auntie Maud. Everyone always sat at the table to eat, every meal time they would sit around the table and discuss their day or just chit chat about anything. Auntie Maud made lovely breakfasts if nothing else, she made lovely pan cakes.

"So, what shall you be doing once school has finished Raine?" Asked Auntie Iris. Raine was not too sure, homework no doubt, maybe a little drawing, writing in her diary. She never did plan her days well. "Maybe we should buy you a planner for Christmas dear, it is good to be planned and not just do things on the spur of the moment." She said into her tea cup.

"But I like that, you never know what surprises could pop up and I would have to say nope, sorry but my planner says I have to brush my teeth." Louie laughed slightly at her reply and pretended to read his newspaper.

"Raine dear, you don't needed to write in a planner your brushing your, oh you are joking again? I never can tell when you are joking." Auntie Iris went a little pink in the cheeks as everyone around the table laughed with a low rumble.

"Still, maybe you should start planning you days, write things down as it were, it could help us in the future when you start going out. We will know where you are dear." Smiled Auntie Pearl, Raine nodded and took her breakfast things to the sink. She smiled brightly and raced to her room, she picked up her readily packed school bag, her coat and drawing pad before running back downstairs.

"I wish you would walk dear." Said Auntie Maud as she almost bumped into her.

"Well I'm off to school now." She said through the kitchen, her Aunties called back their farewells as Louie came out with her lunch. "Thank you Louie." She smiled taking the bag. "I'm off to school now, it will be a long day, I have tech." Louie did his best to smile but failed. "Cheer up Louie, I don't like to see you sad." Raine placed her arms around Louie and gave him the largest hug she could muster that early in the morning. The hug seemed to cheer Louie up as he smiled and returned it just as tightly. Now Raine could go to school happy in the knowledge that Louie, doing whatever job he did, was in a brighter mood that when he woke up. Before Raine left she stood in front of the hallway mirror and made sure her uniform was perfect. She pulled the ribbon in her red hair tighter and walked out of the cottage. The wind blew her fire red hair around her shoulders as she made her way to the village.

It was a peaceful little village full of older people or families with older children. She had not noticed until recently that there were not many young people, Auntie Maud had told her that most left for the big city when they became older enough. She guessed that village life was too quiet and boring for the young people and they decided that life in the big city would be full of some kind of adventure.

Raine often wondered what life was like beyond the small village, she had only seen the city on the television or in books. It did look busy and full of people, but it did not seem to call to her as it did her classmates. They would talk about going to one of the cities, she of course remained quiet, they would talk of the jobs they would go for, the shops they would shop in and the restaurants they would eat in. Of course Raine would stay quiet.

Today was one of the boring days in school, the only class she really enjoyed was technology, and they were building some kind of circuit to make a tablet work without the aid of batteries. Nick Manthers was a quiet young man with glasses and the smartest in her year. He was also, the only person Raine would talk to, then only one who sat with her and the only real one who seemed to understand her enough to know that she did not always like company.

"To create this perfect set of,"

"So Raine, what will you be doing this weekend?" Whispered Nick as Mr Pontoon explained how to make their circuit board. He had such a dull voice, it droned on inside her head like a washing machine on a constant spin.

"Oh, not much. You know my Aunties never let me go that far." They laughed slightly, it was true, they had never let her leave the village on a school trip, never let her go into the valley's or travel into the hilltops and never gave her a reason why. She often got bored of asking why, there was no use to her if all she got was the same replies from each Auntie.

"They do mother you, their worse than my parents. My mother never lets me go outside without my inhaler, she never lets me leave the house without the correct shoes and my father. Well, best not go there." Raine joined in with Nick's laughter, but inside she felt sad, at least he had parents that worried and fussed over him. At least they let him go out and visit the world even if it was just on school trips. Sometimes she liked to forget she had no parents, she liked to think they were at home waiting for her with dinner and a story of their day.

"At least you have the luxury of having a Mother to fuss over you and a Father to, you know." Smiled Raine as they set to work on their circuit board.

School never did feel like hard work, that was until homework needed to be handed in, Raine was not a good home worker and often rushed it or had some kind of help. But she was very good at working hard and blending in with the rest of the school that her school life seemed to fly by her.

Soon it was lunch time and today she decided to stay outside and away from the groups, she retreated to the peace and tranquillity of a nearby bench under a shady tree.

She unpacked her lunch and sketch pad and settled down to her lonely lunch. She seemed to forget where she was as she drew, the other teenagers around her meant nothing to her, their voices, their lives. Nothing made her happier than sitting on her own, eating her home made lunch and sketching. She often found herself doodling something or another, it made her feel so peaceful as she transferred the images from her mind on the paper. Today she was finishing a piece she had been working on for a few days now. There was so much detail that the people looking back from the paper seemed real, she was very proud of their eyes, they almost invited her into the page.

"Hay, weirdo, what you doing?" Sally Grey, the most popular girl in school. She was little miss perfect, her bleach blonde hair was perfect, her gleaming white teeth were perfect, even the creases in her short skirt were perfect. She was the daughter of the dentist, she wanted for nothing but in Raine's eyes she was spoilt with possessions. "Is that homework or are you drawing your little family, give me that." Sally snatched her pad and looked at it, sniggering with her little group of friends.

"It's not homework Sally, I just like drawing."

"Just drawing?" She questioned while her friends looked over her drawing. "And there was me thinking it was some kind of family portrait, oh no that's right." She turned over her shoulder and laughed cruelly. "You don't have a family, just that collection of old grannies and the hot guy. Well, we can't have you disappointing them can we weirdo?" Sally looked back to at her and smirked, Raine looked down and felt her heart break as she began to rip the paper from the pad. "Party tables, cat's wearing suits, even though the guys you drew were quite hot, it doesn't mean you should keep it. Stop reading books weirdo." Sally threw the pieces of paper to the ground and left laughing at Raine with her friends in tow. Sally was such a mean person, Raine never understood why people felt the need to be so cruel to people who were different or did not fit in. "Spec face." She called to Nick as he sped up towards Raine.

"Hello Raine." He was a little out of breath and took his inhaler before sitting down with her. Raine greeted him and knelt down to collect the pieces of her picture, it was ruined, the pad was wet from the grass and the picture was in so many pieces it would take forever to put together again.. "What's that, oh, did Sally do this?" Raine nodded and returned her pad to her bag, she looked at the ruined picture and sighed deeply. "She's just insecure and lonely. I live near her and you know, without her friends she's nothing, in school she is the most popular girl while at home. Well, who knows what the daughter of a dentist does, maybe that's why she goes out so much? And besides, girls like her leave this village, go to the city and get up the duff before you can say pie." That did not surprise Raine one bit. She fought back her tears with her happy thought and returned to her lunch. Nick was very talkative, he spoke about his out of school projects and what he wanted to do over the weekend while Raine sat and ate her lunch, daydreaming of others things until the bell rang for her next lesson. "Oh, well I have a free lesson, study time you know." He smiled trying to make her feel better. Raine waved and left for her next class wishing today would come to an end so she could go back to bed and forget that the day ever happened.

"And the primary message of this piece is communication. Now to the next poem" English. It was a quiet lesson today, they were reading poems, or at least their teacher was, it made her think what they were meant to be learning. The art of poetry or how to listen to a teacher read poetry. This gave Raine time to look out of the window and daydream once more. She liked to let her mind wander away from whatever boring place she was in. School, the doctors, the dentist, sometimes the dinner table. It seem to leave her body and float where ever the wind took it. One day should would day dream about woods while another she was running through a green field surrounded by beautiful flowers. Today she was walking through a grand castle, the poem was about a King sitting high on his throne, lonely without a wife, but that was all she had heard.

As the last bell of the day rang Raine felt her mind fall back into the right place and back to the reality that was beef for dinner. Raine packed up her bag slowly and waited for Sally and her friends to leave the class room before joining the hum of happy students making their way to the main gates.

"Raine, Raine there you are." Nick ran up to her as she reached the school gates, he reached for his inhaler and took three deep breaths before standing upright. "Phew I thought I missed you. I wanted to give this back to you." He handed her a piece of paper covered in tape, Raine looked down at it in wonder. "Open it then." Raine opened the paper and smiled, it was her drawing Sally had torn up at lunch time. He had put it back together, it was back in her hand, all in the right place, it was not finished, but it was back. "It took me a while, but I like puzzles, you're a really good drawer, I know I say it often, but you really are."

"Oh thank you Nick that was such a lovely thing to do for me." She smiled and placed her hand on his shoulder. She was very touched by, what seemed like a small action, but to her it was huge, her drawings were very important to her.

"That's alright, I saw how unhappy it made you and well. Listen, Raine."

"Hmm." She was so happy her picture was back together, she did not think to stick it back together, but here it was, back in one piece. Her mind automatically thought the worst, it was gone, there was no way to put it back together and that was that.

"Tomorrow, would you like to come round my house and,"

Beep, beep.

That car horn, Raine spun around and saw Louie sitting on the bonnet of his car, he waved slightly silently telling her he was waiting for her.

"Oh that's Louie, he's picking me up today, beef for dinner you know. See you tomorrow Nick and thank you again for this." Raine ran towards Louie leaving Nick to go home alone, she knew what he wanted to ask, she had been waiting for it for a while now. Everyone knew Nick liked her, she knew he wanted to ask her out on a date but she did not want a boyfriend. Not yet. "Hello Louie."

"Hello Raine, good day?" Raine smiled and shook her head, they could now drive home and moan about the day they had, they would try and outdo one another on how bad their day was to see who the winner was. It was another one of their little games, this time it was not to test a memory, it was just to sit and moan before they got home. Her Aunties hated to hear she had a bad day.

"Alright, you start." Smiled Louie starting the car.

School life was pretty much the same day in and day out. She would rush into school, she was rarely late but there was always the odd occasion, she would finish her homework, she very rarely missed her homework but again, there was that odd occasion, and she would eat her lunch and listen to the bullies tease her.

"Next month is the village festival, we could like this year to be the best year ever, so we have decided to create a competition." Nick sighed and rolled eyes, he turned to Raine and shook his head, Raine knew Nick hated competitions. He told her that his father often held competitions between him and his older brother and he always lost. He told his sons that a healthy rivalry in academic life would only do them well later in life and while his brother loved the challenge of beating his brother, Nick was happy to just do well without the added pressure. "We shall also have a sports tournament and a beauty pageant, Mr Lauper has said he will arrange the judges for all events. The competition will be artistic based, reverent Hopper has put forward the idea for a competition to design the new stain glassed window for the Sunday school class room."

"You would win that hands down Raine." Whispered Nick with a warm smile, she thought that might be fun to design. She had never thought of using her drawings for design purposes, maybe it could be fun.

"Or he put forward the idea to for participants to create a motive for the walls surrounding the under-fives playground. Something fun, colourful, they have not had a new coat of paint and I think this idea would be lovely." Miss Sweeten began explaining how to enter the competitions and what the possible prises were. Raine was not really interested in prizes, she was never one for winning and did not really care much for it. She liked the idea of people seeing her art work and even making the little children think and maybe have a day dream of their own.

"You could win the art competition, will you enter?" It was very appealing, maybe she would and draw a wood with a river running through it. Or maybe a tea party with all manners of strange creatures around the table. She liked that idea, cartoons, people, creatures with dancing fruit, cake, she had to start writing down the idea now or else she would forget. She loved to draw, it was one of the things she was very good at.

"Home time Raine, you do get lost in your idea's sometimes." Miss Sweeten hovered over her as she jumped out of thought and looked down at her rough sketch. "This is very good, are you going to take part in the art competition?"

"Yes miss, I think I will. Do you think this is good enough?" Miss sweeten had such a lovely smile, she was Raine's favourite teacher in the entire school. She always let Raine know she was there for her with a smile, she often let her mind wander and remind her politely that it was class time and not personal time. She very rarely raised her voice and never once had she told Raine off, she was in her eyes, perfect.

"Yes, I think it could go as far as winning, you really are a good artist Raine, just let that creativity flow more, alright? Now go on, get home." She patted her head and walked back to her desk, no doubt she had lots of work to do. Raine got to her feet and walked over to Nick, who was waiting for her by the classroom door.

"Are you getting picked up today?" yes, Auntie Pearl was picking her up today, 17 years old and she was still being picked up from school every once in a while. Well, nearly every day lately. "Well, I have to go to the library, this homework won't be done by itself, so I'll see you tomorrow?" Raine nodded and waved him good bye for the day. She was very fond of Nick, he was a really nice person and always helped her whenever she was stuck on anything.

"Hello Raine, how was your day at school, was it very productive?" Auntie Pearl was secretly her favourite Auntie of the three. She was so kind and caring, she always gave her sweet things when the others were not looking and spoilt her rotten with hugs and kisses. She was a kindly old lady but very fit for her age, she never once stopped to catch her breath as they almost marched along the village paths.

"Yes, it was fine, a little dull in places." Raine looked up at the hills and wondered if there were many walkers or joggers out today. "Oh Miss Sweeten said there is going to be some kind of art competition this year, either designing the new stain glass window for the church or a wall for kids." Auntie Pearl walked into the small green grocers and began picking out things they needed for dinner.

"Oh well that's nice dear, will you enter? You are a very good artist, why I remember your first painting, it was some kind of tree house in a field with a lovely sunset. I must admit it was very beautiful, like a memory almost. Peas of carrots?"

"Umm, peas." Replied Raine reaching for a fresh bag of peas. "I liked that too, it was just something I dreamt about really. I wish it were a real place, imagine living there." Auntie Pearly hummed her reply, she would love to live in a tree house in the middle of nowhere. The thought of being alone but reachable, the tree would protect her, the grass would be covered in flowers, she could even have her own little garden at the base of the tree.

"You do say silly things at times Raine, sometimes I wonder what goes on inside your head. Louie said he will be home late for dinner, I was thinking we should all sit down together when he gets home and play a board game tonight. What do you think?" That would be a nice idea, it had been a while since they had sat together, maybe it would be nice to talk for a while so she could forget school for a while.

Dear diary,

This entry will be a little different from my usual ones, I'm just feeling a little unhappy, sad, well upset really. Sometimes I just get to the point where I just want to cry because of, well, everything. Friday, the last school day, normally I would be happy at this time of the week, the weekend is nearly here, I don't have to go to school for two whole days and there's no homework left to do. Well at least I think I have no more homework, now I write it I will have to check.

Yet, as I sit here in my room after a really nice dinner, I feel upset. I already have had a good cry into my pillow and had to wash my face after, tears are so sticky. My face was really hot after.

I had a really nice morning and even a nice afternoon, Nick had another awful lunch so I shared mine with him, he's so skinny I think he needs to come and live with us, Aunt Maud would fatten him up in no time. His Mother does try and cook good meals, but she's not very good at cooking, I remember one time she made what looked like a cake, but it tasted so dry I wanted to gag. I often think maybe I should invite him around for dinner, but it might make him think the wrong thing, or maybe he might want to come around more often and then I would never have time to myself.

But that's not really the point of my entry. It was Sally, she was so nasty to me today, it started in PE lesson, and I had to be on her team today for volley ball. Now I'm really not too good at sports at the best of times, but today I was tired and even worse. Our team lost, this gave her the ump I can tell you, she was awful in the changing room, she was ruder still in form class and completely hurtful during lunch.

She said so many hurtful things, she teased me about my eyes, and she even went as low as to mention my parents, saying they left me alone on the old ladies doorstep because I was too ugly. She laughed and added that I was a disappointment to them and rather than go to prison for murder they abandoned me. She found it all rather funny, it raised her popularity but for me, it just hurt, Nick found me crying in my lunch spot. He told me not to let it hurt me, that it was just words and that he never let things like Sally or words hurt him. But he doesn't understand what it's like not to have parents, so many take their families for granted, they have the luxury of hating their parents. They can argue with them, hate them and then make up after. Whereas I, well I have no parents to hate, how can I even curse people I don't know, are they alive, are my Aunties protecting me from something, why don't they ever tell me anything about them?

I don't know what they look like, what their names were, what they did. I do wonder if I look like them, weather I look more like my mother or my father. When I feel down like this I like to think about the people they could be. I like to think my mother had beautiful red hair with green eyes, she's an artist, she free and kinder a hippy. She loves nature and everything around her, she would have a beautiful garden with flowers and home grown foods. Maybe she would have chickens, but she would never kill them, she would find it too hard and it would go against her beliefs. I think she would name them too and remember each one of their names, and I think she would give them a personality. Maybe she's a bit crazy but in a good way, like a woman who loves cats is the local crazy cat lady. She would be the hippy chicken lady.

My father, he's different, he's very wise, maybe a little bit older than my mother, mature, maybe he would have a little bit of grey hair to show his maturity. He would be some kind of business man, not a millionaire, playboy type with no time for his family. The kind of man you think is very scary when he is at work but when he comes home to his earth mother wife and child, he's as soft as a teddy bear. He would be a stern man, I could imagine that he would ground me if I was too naughty, tell me off when I came home or didn't do my homework. But I think he would be the kind of man who would help me when I needed it, he would encourage me to go higher and be who I wanted to be.

Those are my parents in my mind, they are the people I think about when I feel sad about not having real parents, it's a little hard to picture their faces sometimes, but they are there. That image is there to make me feel happy again. Then again, I feel happier after writing this, now I can always go back and read my perfect parents just in case I ever forget them. Maybe I should think of their names, yes, I think that would be fun, it's always nice to have a name to go with faces even if they are made up people. Maybe I could draw a picture of them, the faces I see in my mind should be easy to put onto paper. I do it all the time, why not with my parents.

Here's to the next time I write, I'm sure it will be a lot happier entry.

Saturday. Saturday was Raine's favourite day of the week, the best day apart from Sunday of course. Every Saturday Raine would be the first one up, after having a warm shower and dressing herself she would make breakfast for everyone and then go out for the whole day until the sun went down. She knew every weekend she did this her Aunties would send Louie out to find her, but he never did and that always made her gleeful.

Yet this morning was different, it seemed she was not the first one up, her Aunties and Louie were in the kitchen, they were talking in a hushed tone, she could only just make them out as she walked down the steps. Then, when she reached the door to the kitchen she heard their every word, they were talking about her.

"I can't help but worry, she will be eighteen soon." Came Louie's voice.

"I know how you feel Louie, but we can't keep her in cotton wool, its life, we can't really stop things from happening." Came Auntie Pearl's reply.

"And besides, she's a beautiful girl, and that young Nick is a lovely young man. I talk to his grandmother at the bingo and he will be going places, very high places, she tells me how he wants to make his father's business grow." Added Maud with excitement, she had recently started attending bingo with the other old ladies of her knitting circle. Auntie Maud was so old for her age, bingo, knitting circles, stockings.

"She's too young to have boyfriends. She shouldn't really go out any more, not alone."

"Louie, that's is most unreasonable, I would love to enforce that myself, but we can't, she's not a little girl and heavens know we have tried to keep her within our sights it's just not,"

"Then what shall we do?" Cried Louie, he was getting a little irate it seemed, but without seeing his face she could not tell. Raine wanted to go, but she wanted to stay and listen, she wanted to know why they were talking about her.

"I really don't know Louie, don't you think I have thought about it, we all have. All we can do is advise her, once she reaches eighteen, she'll be an adult. Legally there is nothing we can do," Auntie Iris, she knew the law inside and out, maybe she worked in law in her youth, she never liked to talk about her youth and maybe that was why.

"I still think we should forbid her from going out alone, stop these outings every weekend, stop any after school meetings with anyone, pick her up from school," That was it, she had enough of listening to them talking about her. They were always trying to find new ways of ruling her life, of telling her what to do with it. They were trying to keep her caged like some kind of animal but with no reason other than they wanted to.

But it was her life to use, she should decide what to do with it and how, surely that was the point of growing up and becoming an adult? So, with all the silence of a mouse Raine crept out and made her way towards the only safe path that lead to the hills. She had to leave that house, even though she heard them talking about stopping her, she had to go, she had to get away.

It was refreshing this time of the morning, the early morning dog walkers and joggers of the village ventured this path. She greeted them as they passed her, some knew her from her weekend walks, some knew her Aunties and asked after them but she did not stop to talk for too long. She continued up the trail, higher and higher even passed the dog walkers.

As she traveling higher she liked to think this was her place, high in the hills where not even the teenagers ventured, a place no one ever went but her.

"I would come here every day if I could, miss school and come here, just me on my own" as she walked higher into the hills she began to feel the familiar chill that ran through the place. It never really bothered her, she wore a thick coat and a scarf and buttoned up as she walked. "There it is." Raine stopped at the top of the hill and looked at the ruined castle in front of her.

She had found it quite by accident when she was younger but now she visited it every weekend and whenever she could after school. This was her secret place where no one could find her. As she walked towards it she remembered asking one of her teachers about it. The teacher had told her that it was once a castle, but over time and because no one cared for it the ruins became nothing but a pile of rocks and nothing for people to look at. Thus it was lost to history.

But it was not the ruins she was here for, no, Raine walked through the ruins and over to an opening in the ground that she covered with fallen tree branches, leaves, anything she could find. She pulled them off and looked down. "It still looks so dark." She whispered into the dark opening, she shinned her flash light down and took a deep breath.

Raine had not always been a good climber, in fact she had never been a good swimmer, she was just a normal girl and rather boring at times. She slowly and carefully climbed to the bottom of the opening and shone her flashlight around, to anyone this would have been just a hole with cracked walls and rocks at the bottom. "There." But to Raine it was more, she found the crack that was just big enough for her to walk through and made her way down the very narrow path. The rock either side of her was cool and smooth, she could feel the cold air running through her body as she breath in the rocky atmosphere around her.

Then, the narrow path opened outwards, Raine jumped down into another hole, but this had no opening at the top, it was just a hole in the rocks. The walls were smooth, the ceiling was smoother still, it did not look like it had been carved or fallen in by nature. It was just there, no reason, no marks for why. It was just there.

But Raine knew there was more to this opening in the rock, she began to run her hand over to far side wall, lumps and bumps could be felt, she ignored them, a dip, she ignored that too. "There you are, I always miss you." She said reaching into her pocket. "I sometimes think you move." She shined the light on a small, hand sized trinket of a tree. It looked so real, almost as if the trees swayed in the stillness around her. She could picture birds living in this tree, apples growing, the leaf's growing amber then falling to the ground before growing once again.

With a smile she placed the trinket in the indentation her hand had found, she waited for a moment, holding her breath, waiting, wishing.

<u>Chapter Two</u>

Welcome to Ethernia

The trinket began to glow, Raine smiled and watched as the light from around the trinket began to draw out a door shape in the rock face. She moved her hand away and let the light finish drawing the door, and once it was fully formed she reached for her trinket, her hand clasped over the small tree with excitement.

Raine pushed opened the door and peeked through, she felt excitement as she walked through and closed the door neatly behind her.

"Oh damn, forgot again." Raine opened the door and pulled the trinket out of the rock and swiftly closed the door again, upon which it neatly turned back into rock. She always stayed behind to make sure it sealed itself once more. Raine could not bear the idea that someone else could follow her into this place. It was, after all a secret place only she knew about. "Good morning Poppsie."

"Oh blast my shoes and glasses where ever is that sponge?" Raine laughed and reached for Poppsie's sponge which lay on the floor by his old feet.

"Here you are." She said handing him the sponge, he was always dropping the infernal thing.

"My goodness Madame Raine where did you come from?" Raine laughed had the old door keeper forgotten again how she got through. "Oh yes, yes. I knew that. But you really must announce yourself, I'm not such a young man as I once was you know. How Jerrad expects me to guard the door and windows I do not know." Raine laughed and helped Poppsie to his chair and desk in the middle of the large room. It was nothing special, it had a little mini kitchen in one corner, a bed in another and of course, Poppsie's desk.

"I don't know Poppsie, but it wouldn't be the same if you weren't here to greet me." Poppsie was a lovely old man, but he was not an old man as you and I would think. He was grey haired yes, he had eyes, nose and a mouth. And he had a body, but not the kind of body you or I would have.

"Well, don't just stand there, chop, chop and off you go before I enlist you to wash my windows." Poppsie waved his balloon hand shooing her away and towards the green window. She enjoyed seeing Poppsie every time she came, he would always ask her how she got there. He was the guard, he was meant to stop invaders from coming through the door and into the Room of Windows. But he was such an old balloon now he could hardly stay floating. When she had first met him he could reach the ceiling to clean, but not there were pink and blue cobwebs from the spiders that now lived in the corners. Now Poppsie had to stand on a chair to even reach the top of the window frame.

"The green window." Sighed Raine opened the catch, as she looked over her shoulder at Poppsie trying to swat away a blue spider, she often wondered what lay behind the other four windows. A blue, red, yellow and white always looked inviting to her. "But not today." She would tell herself, and that was what she told herself today as she climbed through the green window and slid down a tree branch until she landed in Wuffle's Wood.

"Raine, Raine, Raine." Sang the small Waffle's she had landed on. Raine looked down and climbed off the long armed Wuffle's. They waved her good bye as she ran towards the edge of the woods, if you or I had slide down a tree branch and landed on a group of square bushes with long arms then we would have run away screaming. But Raine knew the Wuffle's and they knew her, she enjoyed playing hide and seek with them. They were never really good at hide and seek, they were too brightly coloured and never thought to hide in matching coloured places. They would chase her or help her climb the trees. But not today, today she knew what she wanted to do and hide and seek or forest games was not one of them.

She walked through the wood listening to the lovely sounds of Wuffle's wood that you or I would have found strange, but to Raine they were as normal as the birds singing in the trees. It was a very colourful wood, there were no dark spots, only light, and any place that decided to cover the sun was quickly brightened up by a shining light from a small mouse's nose. Raine found it so funny that the little mice just sat in places lighting up the forest. The trees were not the normal green and brown that we know that turn from a lush green to amber then brown. They were blues, greens, yellows, purples and even orange, the body of the trees were all green of course like the grass they stood on.

Then, as she walked out of the forest she finally saw the real field her mind day dreamed to, it was so lush and green, it was beautifully dotted with colourful flowers that seemed to dance in the summer breeze. She loved walking through this field, time seemed to stand still whenever she entered it. She knew every flower, she knew the stream running though it and remembered when she had fallen into it. She knew the bridge that had broken causing her to fall into the same steam, it was very warm and tickled her as she fell in.

"Good morning Raine." The windmill house with the crooked roof and tree house outside, she knew them too. Raine ran up to the windmill with excitement hoping he was there today and not off hunting somewhere.

"Cat, hello how are you?" Cat looked up from his book and removed his glasses with a white paw. He looked very serious and began to bite the arm of his glasses.

"Oh wonderful darling," he said waving his glasses in his hand. "It has been a most productive morning not to mention I have been invited to a party over at Woken Hollow this evening. Oh, it's such fun over there, you really must come one time, although I would have to give you a potion to change you into a creature. A cat maybe?" Raine smiled and sat on the grass as Cat closed his book with a loud thud. He was always reading a book or writing a book, or making some kind of potion from a book.

"No, I think it's safe to say you are the only cat worthy of any party." Cat purred his pleasure, for you or me to see a talking cat would make us think of a good old book. But he was no crazy, stripped cat, no he was a clever Wizard Cat known throughout the land for his magical skills and potions. He was known for his reading and his written word, he was also known for being a tiny bid mad, but more smart than mad.

"Now that reminds me darling. Would you please deliver this potion to the King? Hunter is with him and I did ask him to take it with him. But he muttered something about Pompom's again and clean forgot about it." Hunter was with the King? Well it would be nice to see King Jerrad too thought Raine taking the potion from Cat's paw. "He has been wondering when you would come and see him, the King I mean, Hunter is always talking about Pompom's or you, or Pompom's." Cat walked back into his windmill house, ducking as the arm of the windmill swung around, muttering about Hunter and his crazy thoughts of Pompom's.

"Oh how lovely to see Hunter and the King at the same time." Smiled Raine running towards the edge of the field. She knew that just beyond the field was the castle where King Jerrad lived and ruled over all the land. "It's always a beautiful sunny day here, they never have snow." Thought Raine as she walked happily through the court yard. The hanging baskets greeted her as she walked through the royal gardens, the hedge clippers ran passed her chasing a few rogue berry bushes and the gardeners waved at her merrily. There was always a pleasant smell coming from this garden, it was so light and beautiful Auntie Pearl would have loved it.

"Miss Raine, the King has been expecting you, please go through to the Throne Room." The guards saluted her as she walked passed them. She loved this castle, it was so green and earthy, it felt as if the nature outside did not end, it just happened to walk in one day and set up home within King Jerrad's halls. Ivy ran through the doors and windows and ran all over the walls, it made pretty picture frames and patterns as it ran amuck. The ground was not hard stone or rock, it was soft and bounced like grass.

"But this is the Realm of Terrae, the green and lush land of Earth and it would be rather silly not to have it covered in greenery." Smiled Raine as she heard King Jerrad and Hunter talking loudly about Pompom's. The Throne room was by far the grandest room in the entire castle, it was true the wildness of the green land of Terrae was within the Throne room, but it still had the air and graces that a Throne room should. The throne itself was made from a tree with branch's growing from it, flowers sat around the foot of it and the leaf's changed colour with every visit.

A map of the magical land of Ethernia sat on one entire wall, King Jerrad told her when she first came to visit him he liked to see the entire land, not just his own. She had walked up to it and looked at it on her tippy toes, little figures walked around the map as though alive. He said that his father had asked Cat to make the map come to life, he wanted to see the people of Ethernia as they went about their lives. So every figure represented a person or creature of Ethernia, she had then and still now thought that was pretty cool.

"Raine!" Chirped Jerrad happily getting to his feet, he was dressed in a fine green suit with brown knee high boots today, he never wore a cloak as it made him feel too royal and he hated that. "I just knew you we would see you today, I was pretty sure, or I was certain I'm not too sure, but I knew you would come today." Raine smiled, it seemed he was a little mad today too, some days he was mad, some days he was serious.

"Oh what a lovely day, what a wonderful time in Wuffle's wood, its Raine. We were talking about you only the other day." Smiled Hunter joining Jerrad, he gave Raine a rib breaking hug and took her by the shoulders. "By any chance, have you seen any of those Pompom's?" Raine could see Jerrad roll his eyes with dismay as Hunter went on. "They are dastardly creatures, naughty things that pounce when you have your pants down."

"Whatever are you doing in the woods with your pants down Hunter?" Asked Jerrad offering them all a seat.

"It's best not asked." Said Hunter glumly. "And even best not answered." He was so funny and by far Raine's greatest friend in

Ethernia. She confided in him and told him how she did not fit in, in her own land, that her land was different to his, it was not bright like his, it was not odd like his and it was not crazy like his.

"I think that's the correct thing to say, oh Jerrad I have a potion for you from Cat."

"Oh lovely, I have waiting for this. Have some cake." Offered Jerrad with a smile, Raine loved his Upside down cake and his tea was the best she had ever tasted. "The News Birds were telling me this morning that the Realm of Fire is holding another tournament of some sort."

"Another?" Asked Raine over her cup, Jerrad nodded and reached for the sugar bowl as it jumped to one side.

"Yes, I was invited of course, as a ruler of one of the Realm's I'm often invited to these things. I rarely go of course, they have so many you know. Plus Cat get nervous when they do."

"Whys that then?" Hunter asked dropping his cake on the floor, he looked down at it and shook his head before reaching for another slice.

"Don't you remember what happened the last time they had a tournament?" Even Raine remembered how Cat was stripped almost bare of all things in his garden and cupboards just to keep up the healing potion demands. But Hunter shook his head and began to stare at his cake with suspicion, no doubt he saw something strange inside it.

"Also Poppsie has informed me that the window to the Realm of Air is once again broken, I do not understand what they get up to."

"I blame those Pompom's." Muttered Hunter over his cup, Raine laughed behind hers as he dusted off the crumbs from his stripped suit. Today he wore orange, green and yellow striped trousers with a matching waist coat and a green shirt. He had bad taste in clothes, they never matched and were always the loudest colours one could think of. In fact, he never looked like a hunter at all, at the age of eighteen he had already reached the 'bad dressed dad' stage of his life and would no doubt stay that way.

But then again, he did live in the tree house outside Cat's windmill and Cat had no taste in clothes either unless he was going to a party. Raine had never visited the other Realms so she had no idea if all the citizens of Ethernia were mad or if it was just the Realm of Terrae. "Well, we must not be sitting around eating tea and cake all day when there is a job to be done." Said Hunter jumping to his feet, he pulled Raine up with him and dusted off her cake before bowing to Jerrad. "I can't hunt down all those Pompoms by myself, Raine will be helping me today. You're firing skills are terrible, so today, we practice. Then we hunt for Pompom's. But we need to practice." Raine nodded her reply, she enjoyed learning how to shoot the Floober-Naught with Hunter.

"I will see you soon Jerrad, maybe we can come back later and we can finish talking? Thank you for the tea and cake." Called Raine over her shoulder as Hunter began to run out of the Throne Room with her. She caught Jerrad smile at them with a small wave before they disappeared out of the throne room.

Like all the citizens she had met in Terrae, Hunter had green eyes, he explained that you could always tell where a person or creature came from by their eye or hair colour. His hair was not green, his hair was bright blue, he explained that at times citizen married from other Realms and mixed people came out. He was in a very sensible mood that day and made sense for almost an hour.

"Sometimes it's their skin, they have two colours you know, or they have a mixture of hair and eyes. My Mother was from the Realm of Air you know, they all have blue eyes or blue hair, but none as bright as mine." He had explained, she remembered fondly as they began training with the Floober-Naught how she asked him about growing up and if he had ever seen the lands beyond Terrae. "You know, I haven't, I think it's those Pompom's you talk about, I have to stay here and defend Cat's crops and magical potions from them. By the way, what do these Pompom's look like?" Hunter had asked her too about her home land. It took him a while to fully understand that she was not from any of the Realms of Ethernia. It had taken her a while to understand that once she walked through that door that she was no longer in her world. It was strange to the human mind how one moment it could be in one place, then a completely different place the next.

"Look Hunter, look I did it, I hit Cat's windmill." Hunter jumped in the air and clapped until Cat walked out from his door and looked up at his beloved windmill. His fur began to shiver and he placed his paws on his hips.

"Run for it." Cried Hunter dropping the Floober-Naught. All they could hear as they headed for the Wuffle's Wood was Cat cursing them, telling Hunter that when he gets back he will make him sane.

Cat loved his windmill, Raine felt a little guilty for shooting Floober at it. "But Floober comes off, no worries there, Cat has the bestest cleaning thingies in Ethernia. It's the Naught you have to worry about, lots of scrubbing." Explained Hunter as they walked through the Woods together.

When Hunter had first suggested Raine learn how to shoot a Floober-Nought she thought him even madder than normal. She had never heard of such a toy, but it turned out that it was a real weapon designed by Hunter himself.

"What does it shoot?"

"Isn't that clear?" Raine had shaken her head making Hunter roll his eyes in disbelief. "A Floober is a brown solidy, liquidy thing that goes splat when you fire it from this thingie you see. I have no Naughts so we can't fire them."

"Then why is it called a Floober-Naught if you have no Naught? Wouldn't it just be a Floober?" She had asked innocently, this had sparked one of Hunter's thinking sessions. When Hunter decided to sit down and think it took him hours, he sat down where ever that was and began to scratch his head and hum as his mind seemed to race. Then after many hours of this he snapped his fingers, looked up at Raine who had not long ago woken up from a nap and said.

"Yes it should be, but it's not." Raine liked to remember her days with Hunter, they had such fun every time they were together. Now enough time had passed between the Floober-Naught on Cat's windmill had passed the two felt it was safe to return, and Hunter had run out of Floober to shook.

"Cat?" Called Raine, he was not at his desk.

"Cat?" Hunter checked inside his windmill and shook his head so Raine went around to the garden patch and checked there.

"He's not there." She said, Cat very rarely left the field let alone his windmill. Suddenly Hunter gasped and took Raine by the shoulders and began to shake her.

"Oh no, you don't suppose that the Pompom's came and took him and ate him and then pooped him out and ate him again only to turn him into a Cat looking pile of poop?" He stopped shaking her and looked into her eyes with all the seriousness and hysterics of a mad man.

"Umm. No Hunter."

"Phew." Sighed Hunter letting her go, he looked around and shrugged his shoulders before sitting down on the grass. Where could Cat be, maybe he was out, or with Jerrad, or maybe he was so sad they had fired a Floober on his windmill that he moved away.

"Haaa!"

"ARGH!" Cried Raine and Hunter in unison as a cloud of rain splashed down upon them, it was cold and wet.

"I knew you would come back, ha to you two. Cold are you?" Raine opened her eyes and looked up at Cat as he stood in the door way to his windmill and ducked the arms.

"I'm cold, I'm cold. Raine are you cold? I'm so cold!" Cried Hunter curling up into a small ball, Raine felt she could not speak, the water was so cold it took her breath away.

"Well that should make you think twice about firing Floober's at my windmill ah? Now go and get dried off, you look like two drowned rats." Laughed Cat walking back inside his windmill, Hunter uncurled himself and poked his tongue out at him. "I saw that." Hunter looked to Raine, she was still too cold to even speak let alone wonder how Cat knew Hunter poked his tongue out at him.

"Come inside with me." Hunter took Raine's hand and took her up into his tree house, he light a fire and began pulling out all of his clothes, throwing them on the floor as he searched. "No, too bright, too dull, too big, too small and. Where did this come from?" Then Hunter pulled out his pyjamas and handed them to Raine. "For you until your clothes dry, they are clean Cat washed them all for me." She smiled and took them, she went into Hunter bedroom and changed out of her clothes and into his pyjama's.

She liked Hunter's room, it was simple, there was very little clutter but sadly no photos of his family anywhere. It was very much a boy's room with the unmade bed, clothes all over the floor and the faint smell only a boy could make. "Are you all changed, Cat has some fruit milk for us." Called Hunter, Raine smiled and walked out of his room. "They look nicer on you Raine than they do me, do you have jammie's at home, take those so you have jammie's I would hate to think you have none you see. It gets so very cold." No matter how many times Raine told Hunter she had her own he would not listen and insisted she took his Pyjama's home with her.

"Well, thank you Hunter, now I won't be cold in the night." This made Hunter smile. Cat called them both down from the tree house and stood waiting for them at the bottom.

"Well, for making a mess on my windmill you both have to go and do something for me." Raine did not want to argue, she knew Cat's word was final, he was a very stern cat. "Hunter, go to see the King Wuffle, he has some Wuffle fluff for my potion and Raine. You go to the King and ask for some plum duff for my dinner."

"Ohhh, can't we go together Cat?"

"No you may not Hunter." Snapped Cat crowing his paws, he tapped his paw and waited for them to go. It was not fair, she liked going places with Hunter, but then again they did make a mess of Cat's windmill.

"Ok, Cat, I'll go. If we be superfast Hunter we can be done and come back for more fruit milk." Hunter looked up, then smiled before running off towards the woods. Raine waved goodbye to Cat and ran in the direction of the castle.

She enjoyed her days with Cat and Hunter in Ethernia, she longed to spend more time with them, she wanted to quit school, she wanted to spend nights with them and not just hear about the night in their stories. Maybe she would travel and come back and then stay with Hunter for a while, he always asked if she would stay with him once, but she always had to say no and go back home.

"Raine dear," Jerrad looked her up and down silently question her new appearance.

"Oh, we hit Cat's windmill with Hunter's Floober, we ran away but we did go back after you see. But Cat was still a little mad at us so he wet us with a rain cloud. So my clothes are drying now and Hunter gave me these to wear until then so I don't get cold." Jerrad hummed a little and crossed his arms.

"I do wish I knew, I would have sent more. Lady like attire instead of those. Well whatever Hunter claims them to be." Jerrad was no snob, he never seemed to care what he was wearing unlike most royal people. But whenever Raine looked out of place or, in this case, just plain odd, he liked to try and dress her a little more lady like. He offered her a dress once before, she did take it but ended up tearing it while on one of her expeditions with Hunter. Jerrad was not angry, he laughed and said maybe she should have been born a boy and not a girl. "Come with me, we shall gather Cat's plum duff. It's in the gardens." He said offering her his arm. "So you went to the woods after, what did you do there?" Asked Jerrad as they walked through the castle to the gardens, Raine explained how they talked a little about school and then played hide and seek with a few of the younger Wuffle's. Jerrad was a great listener, he just walked beside her and listened as she told him full of excitement how Hunter stood in front of a flower and thought he was hidden.

"It was so much fun, we played six times I think. Ooh, what's over there, it looks lovely." But Jerrad pulled on Raine's arm stopping her from walking over to a beautiful gate. She looked at him for a moment, he had never pulled her away from something like that before. His eyes sat sadly on the gate as he pulled her along, back towards the gardens.

"There is a place for the royal only, I would take you as my guest but I." He trailed off sadly and returned his eyes to the path in front of them. Raine felt a little bad now, she looked at Jerrad and wondered if she had made him sad.

"Jerrad, did I upset you?"

"Oh dear sweet Raine," Jerrad stopped and took her hand in his own with a kind smile. "No, you could never upset me. That place brings memories to my mind that make me sad, so no little Raine, you did not make me sad. I have to see it every day, so every day I get a little sad."

"Oh, how terrible." That must not be a nice place, and how terrible to have a place that makes you sad so close you have to see it every day. She would hate to have something that made her sad every day in plain sight.

"Yes, and no, it reminds me of things. Then I see this, my beautiful garden and then I remember one does not have to be so sad all the time. See. How can one be so sad with the best garden in Ethernia?" Raine looked to the garden before her, it was indeed the best garden she had ever seen. Granted she had not seen many, but Auntie Pearl's garden was pretty. "Now let us find these plum duff's and fast or else the day will leave us." Raine smiled and helped Jerrad to find the plum duff for Cat's dinner.

Raine's days in Ethernia were very much like this one, she would talk to Poppsie for a while, find Cat reading or writing a book while brewing a potion. She would cause some kind of mischief or another with Hunter and always visit Jerrad for tea and upside down cake. She never tired of doing these things, she never once missed her weekends with them, every weekend was different and every weekend was fun until she had to go home.

"Hunter." Raine looked up at the sky, the sun was rubbing its eyes, for in Ethernia the sun has a face and so did the moon. They did not rise and fall as they do in Raine's world, the moon would come up from where ever it happened to be, shake the suns hand and take its place in the sky, until the sun came back in a few hours and did the same. But Raine knew that when the moon came out, it was time for her to leave Hunter and Cat again. "The moon is on its way, that means I have to go home." She was always sad when she had to leave. Cat looked up from his potion and shook his head, it seemed they shared her feelings too.

"Hunter will walk you to the door, I really have to finish this potion, the green Witch has lost all her green." Raine gave Cat a large hug, which he tried to push away, he hated being hugged and patted like a normal house cat. But she knew he secretly loved being tickled behind his left ear, he would fidget and eventually purr like a contended kitty.

"So, do you think you can come back tomorrow, we have much training left to do and I thought we could go and look for Pompom tracks." Raine never had the heart to tell Hunter that Pompom's were not alive, she had told him how cheerleaders used them in their cheers and he thought them to be some kind of menace. She never had the chance to tell him they were just balls of material that made a rustling sound.

"I hope so, I never really do anything over the weekend apart from visit you." She waved to Poppsie as they climbed out of the green window. Hunter may have been mad but he was a gentleman, he helped Raine from the window and walked her all the way to the rock that was her doorway to her own world.

Raine placed her tree on it and waited for it to finish tracing out the line of a door with the light. "It's those Aunties, and Louie, he's becoming rather, possessive lately."

"Pish and piffle." Snorted Hunter. "Just go home and say, 'Hay, I want to go out and hunt for Pompom's and there's nothing you can do.' Then go out." If only it were that easy, thought Raine sadly. She would love to tell them where she was going every weekend, but she was scared they would think her mad or tell others about Ethernia. "Hay unhappy face, don't look so sad, here this is for you." Hunter threw her a green apple and showed that he had one too. "An Apple a day keeps the Mocter away you know."

"You mean Doctor?"

"Oh course. Those too." Raine smiled and gave Hunter one last hug before walking through her door, she looked over her shoulder and smiled, laughing inside at Hunter's mad smile as he waved merrily.

It was dark when Raine returned to her house, it was still cold and she could feel small droplets of rain touching her lightly on the face. As she reached the back door leading to the kitchen she could hear the worried voices of her Aunties, she could also hear Louie telling them she should never be alone and that it was high time she stopped going out alone. That would be terrible, if they knew about the door to Ethernia.

"Where have you been Raine, we have sent Louie looking everywhere for you, we thought the worst for a while." The moment she set foot in the door her Aunties descended on her. Auntie Pearl was first, she always started to rub any dirt from her face with her lace hankie, while Auntie Iris took her coat and made her a hot drink. Auntie Maud stood with Louie and crossed her arms ready to tell her off for leaving without a note or telling them where she had been. It was always the same although recently Louie was joining in by telling her off.

"I was out near the hills, it was a nice day and I wanted to go for a walk, I guess I lost track of time, but I do have lots of things to draw." She explained, but it seemed that Louie was beside himself with anger as he did not let Auntie Maud talk.

"I walked all around that path three times, we have been worried sick. You could have fallen, got lost, been taken. Who knows what could have happened." He said sternly.

"Well, I'm sorry. But I'm fine see, not a mark on me." Her Aunties looked at one another silently exchanging messages no one but they could hear. Louie held his head in one hand and turned his back, Raine could not understand, she was unhurt. They knew she went out alone to the hills walking, they knew she always came home safely, sometimes a little late but always safe.

"A nice young man knocked for you today, we had to tell him you were out doing some art home work. What was his name?" Auntie Pearl changed the subject and ignored Louie's harsh breath. "Nick? He is a very nice young man." He was, but she knew what he wanted, she wanted to change the subject now.

"You weren't with him all day were you?" Asked Louie looking over his shoulder.

"I'm going to bed." Said Raine pretending not to hear Louie, she was in no mood for his silly questions. "I'm very tired, I don't think I will have dinner." She said running up the steps, but Louie followed her to the bottom of the steps trying to continue the conversation, but she did not stop.

Raine raced to her room and closed the door, she could still hear them all talking about her behaviour today and how could they keep her in check. They always did that now a days, how can we keep her inside more without taking away her freedom said Auntie Pearl. While Auntie Iris would side with Louie and say sometimes creatures did better in captivity and Auntie Maud would offer them all tea or coffee.

But this never bothered Raine, in her mind she was happy providing they never found out where she really was. If anyone were to ever know about everyone in Ethernia, she shuddered at the thought of the rest of the world knowing there was a door to another world. Her world. After getting into her night clothes Raine reached under her mattress for her secret diary, she flicked through the pages and read some of the entries. They were all about Ethernia, she had drawn lots of pictures to go with the entries. She smiled at some of the adventures Hunter had taken her on, the horse rides Jerrad had shared with her, she had even added the stories she had heard from Poppsie. He was as old as the hall of window's and had many a tale to tell. He could name every King or Queen who had sat on the throne, he could even remember the day Cat was born.

"But I can't remember how long ago that was, but I do remember the day." He had scratched his head and tried to think about the day, but even when Raine had returned to go home, the thought still eluded him.

"Maybe I'll read some old entries, sometimes they are better than books." Smiled Raine flicking though the pages of her diary, she wanted to relive something, anything to make her forget about school, life, everything. "Oh I remember this one."

Dear diary,

I had another crap day at school, no doubt it will only get worse after the weekend because I ran away from the school gates. It really upsets me that I'm bullied, it's sad, but confusing. It confuses me that because someone is different they should not only be shunned but teased. I think being different should be celebrated, different is unique.

Jerrad agrees with me of course, I went to visit him today, Cat told me Hunter had left early to hunt Pompom's again. Jerrad said he found it hard to believe someone like me was ridiculed for only having different eye colour, I think that word means teased, I might look it up or ask Louie, he's very clever sometimes. I told him that people in my world had the same colour eyes, that brown, blue and green was the norm for us and that anything different was considered strange. Even my bright red hair is odd to some people, some like it where as others find that it looks out of place. Personally I have always liked my hair and eyes, it's nice to be different, but it does make social life a problem. In my world at least.

Now where was I? I do get so side tracked sometimes and forget what I was saying, I wonder what I will think when I read this back in years to come? Yes, I spend today with Jerrad, it was really nice, he decided to take the day off from his royal duties and take me for a long walk through the castle grounds. We went through the green house where the food was being grown, being Ethernia it was not normal food like carrots. I think that's what I like about it, like I always write, everything makes no sense when your back in this world, but when your there it makes all the sense in the world. Jerrad told me that his favourite food to eat was something called a Goot, we dug one up and I took one bite and thought it tasted like dog food. It was so gross I really can't understand how he can eat it, he just laughed at me and carried on eating his own. He did add that it was an acquired taste and was better once cooked.

Jerrad also has the best apple trees in Ethernia, I think it has something to do with the earth. There are so many colours, not just red and green, I really like the pink apples, they are very sweet while the blue have a little sourness to them. I thought about them as I walked home, Jerrad tends to the trees himself you see, he told me he does nothing to make the apples change. He said that the trees make their own mind as to what colour apples they grow, one year every tree in the castle produced brown apple which tasted very bad, Cat used them in his potions apparently. I really don't know what he could have made. Knowing Cat it was something useful, or horrid.

Further in the grounds we wandered to a brook, Jerrad introduced it as a babbling brook, now to make this clear, this brook was not babbling like a normal brook back home. The water crashing over rocks and washing up on the bank, creating that sound that makes you want to go for a wee all the time. Nope, I had to kneel down to be sure and even ask Jerrad if what I was hearing was right, he laughed and asked what did our brooks do if not babble. His brook was actually babbling, not sentences that made any sense mind, but so many voices talking so many words it created such a din. Even now sitting in my room I wonder where the voices were coming from.

Cat came by after a few minutes, he was collecting babbles for a potion he was working on. He greeted us and told Jerrad that the Blue Witch had lost her voice again and he had to make yet another potion to help her. It seemed from their conversation this Witch lost her voice often. Cat explained over dinner that night that she often puts her voice down and forgets where she last left it, after the tenth time of losing it her voice decided it would no longer call out to her and it would just sit where ever she left it until found. He also added that his potion babbled and encouraged her voice to come back, he muttered that one day she will lose her voice and it will never come back, he was sure it would up and leave, never to return. I found that very funny, but it seemed like a serious problem that always happened. But it was still funny to me.

Dinner was really nice, Jerrad gave us a feast of jellies, apple and other fruits, he said he felt like a sweet, juicy dinner so not one bit of meat was in sight. Hunter was a little late but still dressed as bright as ever. He sported a yellow suit today, it was a little grubby at the knees and elbows but he still looked very nice. I wish I could be so carefree and not worry about what I looked like. But I think with burning red hair and two different colour eyes is enough. Cat kindly brought lots of fruit milk for dinner, Hunter loves the stuff, Cat was forever finding him in the cupboards looking for it and was forever chasing him up to his tree house.

Hunter told me he put up some new moss in his tree house, in his bathroom. He's very proud of his tree house, I've been in there lots of times, I'm sure I've written about it. It's really nice and really cosy, I wish I could live with him, or maybe in one next door, or in the same tree above. He told us how he was tracking some odd looking foot prints in the Wuffle's wood, he followed them for hours and eventually they lead him to Cat's windmill of all places. It turns out Cat had been in the wood earlier that morning and forgot to wear his shoes, Hunter has never seen Cat's paw prints and thought they might be the prints of a Pompom, I still haven't the heart to tell him that Pompom's are not real, but it seems to make him happy. Plus Cat tells me Hunter no longer gets lost outside of the forest and never hurts himself, so that's good.

I really wish I didn't have to go home sometimes, I fell so happy in Ethernia, Cat and Hunter are such good friends, even Poppsie when he tells me off for running is dear to me. And Jerrad, he makes me feel like I'm a member of his family, he gave me an apple to take home today, but I mustn't let anyone see it, its purple and I think people might ask questions. Well, I'm going back again tomorrow, Hunter said he found a babbling brook in the castle grounds and he wanted to show it to me, I could only laugh really, I didn't want to tell him that I already knew it was there. He was so excited he told me three times.

Until next time

Raine laughed, Hunter was so funny, that entry was last year but it seemed like yesterday as she relived the babbling brook. She had visited it again with Hunter, he was so excited that day, he had the habit of repeating himself many times when he was excited. The only problem was he got so excited that he fell into the brook, Raine was all but ready to jump in after him, but the brook cursed at him in one loud voice and Hunter was thrown out. They had returned to Cat, Hunter was dripping from head to toe, but Cat refused to let him come in and cover his carpet in water.

"I don't mind you coming in darling, but he has to stay outside, I will not have wet human smell in my house." Hunter did stay outside, even when it rained he stayed outside, but Raine could not leave him alone, she raced out and began running in the rain so she too was wet through. Cat had no choice but to let them both in after that. He never liked to admit it but he was a softie really and could never stay stern for too long.

"Happy days." Raine snuggled down into her covered and decided to go to bed, she was tired, it was nice to read back over her days with Hunter, Cat and Jerrad. "But if anyone was ever to read them, I'll just say they were dreams or something." Thought Raine to herself as she turned her light off. There was very little doubt in her mind that anyone could find her diaries, they were under her mattress until they were full, then she put them under a loose floor board for safe keeping. No one knew about the floor board, the loose floor board near the window. That was her secret place.

"Raine," Nick sat beside Raine again for lunch, he pulled his bag off and began looking through it for his lunch. "You were late for school today, what happened, you're never that late." She had over slept, she was having such a nice dream about flying over a sea she could not wake up. "I never over sleep, I go to bed early, after my homework and dinner of course, then bright and early I'm up and awake ready for the day." Nick smiled and looked at his lunch, it was sandwiches again, he looked so disappointed as he put them down on the table with a thud.

"Do you want some of my lunch, Auntie Pearl made dinner today so there's loads."

"Are you sure, I don't want to take your food if you're eating it." She never ate all of the food when Auntie Pearl made her lunch, she could not eat that much food. Raine was not fat, but she was not stick thin either, she liked to eat, but not that much.

As she shared her lunch between them she thought about all the other students eating the dull looking food from the school kitchens. Home cooked food was always the best, Nick agreed with her, he said that

Raine must have the best cooked lunch not only in the school but in the village. She often wondered why Auntie Pearl did not open a small café or place to eat as she was a very good cook.

There was only a few that would have home lunch, Nick and Raine was two of them and often shared or swapped lunch. It was strange, Nick was the only person who really spoke to Raine, he was so kind and open, he was often bullied himself for being smart.

"I don't understand why being smart is a bad thing." Jerrad had told her that bullies always picked on things that made them jealous, he made his explanation a lot more intelligent sounding, he was so well educated Raine sometimes felt dumb. But this lack of understanding on the bully's part had given Raine a friend and someone to talk to during some lessons and most breaks.

"We have an exam soon, I'm dreading it." Said Nick looking over his timetable for today.

"I know, I'm not looking forward to it myself, just imagine when the big ones come along," Nick grimaced and snapped his timetable shut.

"I dare not, I heard that the papers were late to come through the post last year because Mr Crouch forgot to open the doors for the postman from the city. I would hate to wait like that, I just want to get it over and done with." But Nick was smart, he was the highest achieving student, not only in her class or year, but the entire school. "Have you decided what you want to do when school is over?" She had not really thought that far, she only ever thought about her next trip to Ethernia. Maybe she should travel and see this world, but maybe she should go with Jerrad on his royal visits, where ever that might be.

"I don't know, I haven't really thought about it, travel and draw?" She shrugged, Nick began to explain how he wanted to take over his father's business and maximise the takings, expand and grow further afield. "Maybe I can tell Auntie Pearl about Ethernia, then she could pretend that I'm traveling around the world or something. Then maybe I could have that sleepover Hunter has been wanting." She smiled deeply as she thought about all the fun Hunter had planned for their sleep over. Hunter had no one to spend the night with either, he had Cat, that was his best friend but he lived below and never wanted to climb the tree. He told him that Wuffle's sometimes came into his tree and woke him up, or small Gnomes broke in to steal his hats. But he was very much like Raine, a little bit of a loner, but he always had Cat and Jerrad so he was never really alone. "I wonder what you're all doing right now." Hunter was so lucky, he did not have to attend school, Cat had tried to school him many years ago, but with Hunter's long thinking habits and tendencies to forget things, Cat slowly gave up and decided to let him get on with things in his own way.

Jerrad on the other hand had enjoyed school, he was taught by the smartest professor in the land, he still visited the old man to learn anything new. Raine hoped she could grow up like him one day, he seemed to know the answer to most things and whenever she asked something he did not know, he would find out and tell her the answer next time they met. It seemed to Raine that a ruler had to be very wise no matter how young they were, Jerrad was not old, he looked young and fresh and she often wondered why he had no Queen.

"I have no time for dancing with young women, I have an entire land to run and things to learn, plus the only lady in my life right now is you. And I must do my nest to entertain you, must I not?" Raine was happy she meant so much to Jerrad, it was like having a big brother or uncle looking after her, advising her or telling her off for leaving her home without a word.

"So, what do you think, epic right?" What was epic? Raine had drifted off into her thoughts again and had quite forgotten Nick was there, talking about his ideas for his father business. He looked at her as she tried to remember something, the smallest detail, but nothing came. "You was day dreaming again. Whatever am I to do with you Raine?" She was grateful Nick was such a kind person, he never seemed to mind when she drifted off, although she knew it was very rude of her to ignore him like that. "Well, I must say, your Aunt Pearl is a great cook, you really are so lucky to have such a great cook in your house, my mother is a terrible cook you know." They laughed together, Raine had never been to Nick's house, he had met his mother and father during a village party and they seemed very nice. A little plain and very quiet, but really nice people, they had told her that Nick would talk about her and offered her to come around for dinner one evening, yet she had never taken them up on the offer.

"I never cook, no one lets me so I can't tell if I can cook well or not. It that important when you're an adult?" Nick seemed to think, it did not really matter to her if she could or could not cook, she knew one Auntie would come to her home with food. They just seemed that way, even if she moved out, she would never really be without them.

"No, not really, providing old man Marley doesn't close the pub anytime soon, we should be fine." That was true, old man Marley had the best pie in the village. Tuesdays was the best night and the pub was always full with people wanting his pie and mash. Even Louie loved it, he would take Raine down there every week secretly for dinner and tell Auntie Maud that they were not hungry, she always cooked on a Tuesday. Auntie Maud was not the best cook, she was rather harsh with food, she beat it until there was nothing left of it. Raine laughed to herself and thought of a cavewoman making dinner in the same fashion.

Maybe it was time to learn to cook something, maybe start small with a cake or cookies, that would be nice because she could take them to Jerrad for afternoon tea. Then again, no one could cook as well as Cat, his cake and tea was the best. She would ask him, Cat was always happy to explain what he was doing and this should not be any different.

"I was thinking about going to the library Nick, I have a few things I need to look though for homework. Want to come, or are you busy?" Nick was never busy, his homework was always finished and he always offered to help Raine with hers. He even told her if she was ever that stuck he would do her homework for her, but she would never do that, she would never cheat, not even for good marks. After all, if she never finished her homework today it would not be the first time, she tried hard but her visits to Ethernia felt more important to her, she liked to have fun there more than sitting at home or in some library writing boring things just to make her teachers happy. So it was often a last quick visit to the school library after a bite to eat, finish the home work and then back to her class where she hoped it was correct and did not look too rushed.

Dear Diary,

I had a little argument with Louie today, for some reason we have been clashing and it's not very nice when we do. But he makes me so mad sometimes I just can't help myself. You see Nick walked me home today, I thought it might be nice to accept his offer for once, he often makes the offer to walk me home you see but I never take it, I like to walk alone when I'm not being picked up.

Well the argument today was because of Nick, Louie must have over heard us talking about the festival, I entered it you know, the school decided that we should design a mural for the children's playground. But anyway, Nick walked me home, when we got there he started acting very strange, he asked me if I wanted to come around his house for dinner and to watch a movie. To be honest I would like to spend more time with him, but not for the reason he wants. I have a feeling he has a crush on me, so if I was to say yes that would make him think that I liked him in that way too.

But it's hard because I just like him as my friend, we are and always have been the bullied ones in school, but I guess we're growing up and boys do tend to have crushes, then again so do girls but I don't have a crush on anyone, that's why this diary is so boring.

Anyway, when I got in Louie asked me what was Nick doing talking to me like that, I told him he just wanted me to visit him for a meal and movie with his family. But Louie seems to think the same as me, he went on about how boys his age only have one thing on their minds, how he would brag if anything was to happen between us, he would laugh behind my back to his friends. But he doesn't know that Nick has very few friends, in fact I have never really heard him speak about any of his other friends.

Then he had the cheek to ask me if I understood what happens between girls and boys. I was rather offended not only because he thought I was so blind not to know, but that he would even think about lecturing me on the birds and the bees. Besides, Auntie Pearl already told me all about growing up and sex so there's nothing for him to worry about. I have no intention to have sex with anyone let alone Nick.

But Louie didn't let me get a word in either way, he went on about how boys wanted to use girls as trophies to show off to other boys, that once they had their way they dumped the girl and moved on to the next pretty thing. To be honest he has no right to talk about Nick that way, he's a lovely young man and I'm sure when he finds the right girl who likes him too, they will have a lovely relationship.

But enough about Nick and bad tempered Louie, I did something very naughty today, I left home before dinner and went to visit Jerrad. I know it was a silly thing to do because it made every one worry but I really wanted to get out and away from that place. School and Louie had made me so mad I wanted to scream, but I thought talking to Jerrad would calm me down and cheer me up.

It was late when I reached the castle, Jerrad already had his dinner and was relaxing in the library with Cat when I arrived. They were very happy to see me, Cat noticed that I looked rather flushed, I told him that I had been running through his field again.

"Whatever possessed you to do such a crazy thing like that darling?" He had asked me. I told him there was no real reason, I just felt like running. I feel so alive whenever I'm in Ethernia, there's something about the place that makes me feel like I can run forever, the air makes my body feel alive with such energy I really can't put my finger on what it is. "That sounds like something Hunter would say." Cat never sounded bitter about Hunter's activities, he sometimes sounded like he was disappointed. When I told him that I wanted to see new places and draw he said he wished Hunter would do something constructive. To be honest I could imagine Hunter replying that Pompom's needed to be hunted and he was the only one to do it. He always says something silly like that.

Jerrad was very nice, while I was talking with Cat about his new carrot patch he went to the kitchens and made me some dinner. He is a very good Chief for a King, he never seems lazy like most royalty, I have read about some prince or princesses that have people who wait on them hand and foot. Jerrad had laughed when I told him about those and said he would never do that, he always let his staff in the castle stop work after the sun swaps with the moon. I always wonder where the sun goes, I mean, the map on Jerrad's wall is flat like ours, but I have never asked him if Ethernia is round like a globe. To me it would make more sense if Ethernia was round, then it would mean that the Sun went to the other side while the moon did it. This place is so crazy it might be square for all I know.

After a nice talk with Cat and Jerrad Hunter burst in, he looked very hot and bothered, he ran over to us and sat down with a flop.

"I can't stand gnomes I can't stand them." I could not help but laugh at him, to me gnomes are little garden ornaments, but here they are little things that wake him up at all hours of the morning with rude words and at time, buckets of water. Cat sighed and noticed Hunter was wearing his pyjamas, they were decorated in leafs and trees. They were very nice, I quite liked them. Hunter went on to tell us that he was in bed and three green gnomes woke him up and chased him all around Cat's field. Cat mentioned that he was considerably taller than the gnomes and he should learn to stand up for himself. But Hunter explained these three were bullies, I knew how that felt to be bullied, but I never said anything, I just patted his shoulder.

I don't know how long we stayed in the library but it was very nice, I can't remember ever feeling so relaxed while at home. It's sad to think or even say it but I really like being at the castle with Jerrad, Cat comes to visit, Hunter is always popping in and out with some kind of crazy story. I think if my Aunties were to ever read this diary and see how much I really care about Jerrad they would feel very hurt, to know that I like being with someone that's not in my family would be very hurtful. I hope they never find out, I mean I might tell them one day.

Jerrad took me to the door, he said he wanted to stretch his legs. I have always felt I could talk to Jerrad about anything, it's strange really, I have spoken with him about things I have never told Auntie Pearl, and I'm very close to her. I told him how I get bullied and about my argument with Louie. He told me not to worry, he said that it sounded like Louie was a protective person, he must care about her deeply and simply wanted to ensure she was taken care of. Jerrad then did something odd, he asked me if I liked this person, Nick, he asked if he could be someone I wanted to marry and have a family with. I just laughed and said no, I was only young, I wanted to be free for a little while longer. Plus I told him that although Nick was a very nice person he wasn't the kind of person I wanted to be with. He nodded and said that was very wise, he also told me that rushing into relationships was never a good idea, that a Union of hearts and souls should be with someone you know and care for. I thought he was very deep, he was very loving as he spoke about relationships. I wish Louie had been this way instead of just shouting and going into gross things like sex.

When I walked home I knew I was going to be told off, I knew Louie would be there or close by waiting to shout at me again. I don't really want to go into what happened when I came home because I had such a lovely time in Ethernia. Jerrad said we could go for a walk when I go back, but Hunter wants to take me to the babbling brook again, I think he forgot we have already been there.

Well that's it, until next time.

Raine looked at her page, her hand was aching a little after the long diary entry, she smiled warmly. This was her secret, this place would be her secret until she was old enough to leave home, maybe she would ask Cat if she could live with him until she and Hunter made her a small hut at the foot of his tree. They had joked about that so much but lately that joke seemed more like a good idea, at least she felt at home there, she had friends and adventures she could never have here in the valley.

But that was enough writing for tonight, she would try her best to go and see everyone again, if not she would visit after school and tell them she was doing homework again.

And that was Raine's life, she would get up, go to school, get ignored or teased by Sally while Nick tried to comfort her. Then she would return home to her doting Aunties and stern Louie for a homemade meal before spending her weekends and sometimes evenings in Ethernia. This life may have been strange, but it was hers and she liked it, she knew deep in her heart there was something missing. She wished that gap could be filled by her parents, but Auntie Maud, Iris, Pearl and Louie were her family, and Cat, Hunter, Jerrad and all the other people and creatures of Ethernia were her friends. At that moment as she closed her eyes to go to bed, she could not be happier.

Chapter Three

Foggy Island

"But I'm nearly an adult, what are you going to do, keep me locked up here until I'm an old lady? What if I want to go running through a wood hunting Pompom's?" Cried Raine passionately.

"Pompom's?" Iris looked to Pearl and Maud who shrugged their shoulders.

"Or what if I want to go and live at the foot of a tree with a windmill as my only sight and a mad Hunter living in the tree?"

"What madness are you talking about?" Raine felt so hurt, she was so upset by all this fighting. It had been going on for days, recently she and Louie were arguing more about her going out alone.

She wanted to continue to go out while he wanted her to stay in or have someone go out with her, her Aunties took the same opinion but not as strong as he. "Don't you walk away from me young lady, we're not finished."

"Stop talking to me like you're my Father because you're not!" Shouted Raine, she turned away from the four of them and ran out of the kitchen. She could hear Auntie Pearl calling for her to come back, but she did not want to.

Raine ran passed the school path and towards the hills, she felt tears rolling down her face as she ran passed the dog walkers, passed the joggers.

Why was Louie was mean to her, what had she ever done but try and please them by working hard at school? She had never been in trouble, she had never done anything wrong and never once answered back. Raine was always at the dinner table for Sunday lunch and always there for breakfast. She helped Auntie Pearl with the gardening when she asked and carried the shopping once a week when Louie could not drive them to the market. "I don't know what to do, why is it so unfair?" She thought to herself, wiping the tears from her eyes as she tried to open the door to Ethernia.

So she went out, she always came home safely, she never came home at the early hours of the morning and she always said she was sorry. She could not understand why things were getting worse, why Louie was becoming so unreasonable. Ever since she turned seventeen things started to get tighter, Louie became sterner and more controlling.

Raine ran to the green window and made sure she did not wake Poppsie, she knew he would tell her off if he found out she had skipped school. But she did not care, she did not want to go to school, she wanted Hunter, or Cat, or Jerrad. Anyone of them, all of them. One of them.

Raine slid down the tree and fell into the Wuffle's, they gathered around her as she lay in their comfortable bodies, looking at her as she curled into a ball and began to cry.

"Pompom!"

WHACK!!!

"Ouch!" Now she really had something to cry about as she held her head as it began to throb.

"Oh Hunter look at what you have done." As Raine opened her eyes she looked up and saw Cat pushing Hunter into a nearby puddle before walking over to her. "There, there dear there is no need to cry, there's not even a bump in sight you see. Whatever are you crying for?"

"I hit her in the head that's what, what." Hunter began to wring the puddle from his clothes, it shook a watery fist at him before sliding off into the woods. Normally something like that would have made her smile or at least laugh, but she turned her head away and wiped her eyes. "I didn't hit you that hard did I?"

"No, you made my eyes water a little, but no."

"Whatever is the matter darling?" Asked Cat as Hunter, rudely plopped down beside him. He took his shoe off and began taking out implements for making a cup of tea while Cat muttered unspeakable words.

"It's my family, well my guardians. They won't let me out alone, their being so mean to me and I've done nothing bad. If they won't let me out alone then I can't come here you see. I really do try and make them happy I really do, and I don't want them to stop me from coming here to you."

"Oh that is a predicament."

"How?" Asked Hunter taking a deep drink from his cup. "Yuck. Cheesy."

"Well think about it Hunter, I may not be the smartest Cat in Ethernia,"

"Yes you are though." Cat coughed and continued pretending not to hear Hunter's interruption.

"IF, Raine's guardians were not to let her go out alone, she could not cross over from her world to ours." Hunter scratched his head and thought for a moment leaving Cat to sigh deeply and shake his head.

"That means, Hunter, she would not see us anymore and vice versa." Hunter hummed as he took in all Cat's words, he seemed to sum them up before lifting a finger and asking plainly.

"What's a vice versa?" Raine could not help but laugh as Cat placed his little furry face in his paws and shook his head. Even in her unhappy mood, she knew Hunter would cheer her up with his silly ways.

"Why do I even bother, I really can't understand why I even try sometimes." Cat got on all fours and began walking away, his mutterings could be heard even when he was out of sight.

"Guess what?" Asked Hunter suddenly grabbing Raine's hands.

"You found Pompom's?"

"Oh gosh no, they still are avoiding me, do you suppose they are scared of me? Most likely. But guess what? Oh I asked you that didn't I, or did I? Oh, guess what?" Raine smiled and played along with Hunter's silly game. "I have something to show you, I found it on one of my explorations, it's so very nice and exciting I just had to show you. I was telling Cat before I thought you was a Pompom you see. Such naughty little creatures, have you ever seen a Pompom?"

"Hunter," He had got side tracked again, he was forever letting his mind run away with him, he forgot to stop sometimes and take a breath and Raine would have to take his face in her hands, tell him to stop and breath. "What did you find that you wanted to show me?"

"Oh yes, I found something while exploring. Come on I'll show you." Hunter pulled Raine to her feet and dusted her off. "You are so very dusty." He was very light as he brushed the dirt off her, he pulled out a hankie and wiped her face. They were about to run out of the woods when Hunter stopped suddenly and turned to Raine with a serious look on his face. "Raine."

"Yes Hunter, what is it?"

"Please don't cry anymore, you're so very pretty when you don't and it makes me want to be sad and I don't like to be sad. And I don't like you to be sad." Raine smiled. "That's better. Now off to the exploration we go post haste." And with that Hunter almost pulled Raine's arm off and ran out of the wood.

Together Raine and Hunter ran out of the wood and into Cat's field, they ran passed him and passed the road leading to the castle where Jerrad was no doubt doing more royal duties. They ran and ran until Raine felt quite ready to burst from the inside until Hunter stopped so suddenly that Raine fell into something wet.

"Whatever are you doing in the water?" Asked Hunter as she came to the surface, Raine looked at him and slashed water at him a little annoyed.

"You let go without telling me, so I carried on running and landed in the water."

"Oh. Ok." Raine tried to stay annoyed at him to prove a point, but Hunter was so scatty she found it was a futile exercise. "Look, look over there, that's what I found, you see it." Raine turned around and looked at whatever Hunter was pointing at.

It was a little misty at first, but the more she looked the clearer it became. It was an island, a very grey and lifeless looking island in the distance. She could not make out any landmarks or people, in fact she could see nothing but outlines. "I found a boat, so I really don't know what you're doing in the water Raine. Did you want to swim. By the way, why am I wet too?" Raine shook her head and climbed out of the water, she pushed Hunter slightly and got into the boat. She guessed Hunter was going to take her over to the island the moment he pulled the boat over to her. "You are so very clever, I thought we could explore it and name it and have adventures on it and. Raine, why are you wet?"

"Hunter, let's go." Hunter nodded with a bright smile and began to row the boat through the water. It was very misty as they got closer to the island, it looked like fog, but there was no cold to it. Raine explained what fog was to Hunter he had never seen it before today.

As the boat sailed softly over the water, Raine looked over at the lifeless island, it was cold looking, but there was a warm breeze in the air. She felt her troubled beat softly as she turned back to Hunter rowing the boat. He was so excited, his face never seemed to have any troubles. She wondered, sitting there, if Hunter ever had a bad day, weather he ever felt the world was a sad place or weather his life was nothing but fun and games.

"Land hoe by Joe. I wonder who Joe is." Questioned Hunter as the boat hit the bank of the island, it was still strangely warm for and island covered in fog. Raine and Hunter got off the boat and stayed close together as they walked away from the bank and deeper into the fog.

It was so quiet, there was no wind, no trees, no birds, it looked like a ghost island, but Raine never told that to Hunter, there was a chance he had never heard of ghosts and think they were just as dangerous as Pompom's. For some reason she did not want Hunter to come to this place alone, at least now they had one another to look after the other.

"What a strange place, where do you think we are?"

"Well, I don't think its Terrae anymore, there's not one bit of green any place." She had noticed that too. "Oh no, scary things." Hunter pulled Raine close to him and turned around as a large thing came into view, it made no sound, the ground did not rumble. Nothing happened.

She stayed in his arms for a few moments, waiting. Raine peeked over Hunter's shoulder, surely it was safe enough to have a small peek.

"Hunter. Look."

"Has the scary thingie gone?"

"Hunter, it's not a scary thing, look it's a playground. Or at least it was a playground." Hunter turned around and looked. She was right of course, it was a deserted playground, parts were broken and covered in fog, but it was a playground none the less. There was slides going up and down, swings sat dotted around the place, there was horses, pigs, everything a child could ever want to play on but all faded, all broken and void of any life.

"Where's all the colours gone, it's very strange to have a place with no colours you know, very strange." Said Hunter sounding almost sane.

"Whys that?" Hunter looked at her very seriously.

"Well, Cat said that all the Realms of Ethernia have colours, that they are bright and loud and they represent their land. But to have a place with no colours is just scary, is it like this where you come from?" Raine shook her head as she walked around the playground, it was so sad to see such a lovely place so colourless and foggy. "Maybe this mist took all the colour away." Maybe, she did not know much about the workings of Ethernia, she did not know much about the lands apart from Terrae. Maybe this place was once beautiful, maybe because there was no people there was no light, if any one would know it would be Cat. Maybe they should ask him when they got back. "Let's dance." Said Hunter brightly.

"What?" But Hunter did not let her speak, he took her hands and pulled her close and began to dance with her. As they spun around and danced Raine could not help but laugh with him, she had almost forgotten her troubles at home. "Ouch my foot."

"Sorry." They continued to dance until they came to the remains of what looked like a castle, it was still very foggy and neither could see the floor that well. "Raine," said Hunter twirling her around in circles.

"Yes." She felt a little dizzy as he stopped and pulled her back again.

"Why don't you visit me every day, why is it so long between visits?" That was hard to explain, he knew about her school life and how important it was to go to school. But how could he ever understand Louie and her Auntie's wishes? Did she really understand that her world was different from his and it was not that easy to leave? "Well, I'm just glad you come that all." Hunter took both her hands in his and began to spin around until he lost his footing. They both fell on the floor, Raine fell on her back and Hunter, who had not let go of her hands, fell right on top of her. "Oops, I forgot to let go." He said looking down at Raine.

She smiled brightly and wiped off a small patched of dust from his nose. She then had a desire to kiss him on the cheek, she did not know why, she had never wanted to kiss Hunter before, but something made her want to lean forward and kiss his cheek. "Oh, what was that for?" He asked full of surprise as he softly kissed his cheek.

"I don't know, fun?" Raine shrugged as Hunter seemed to think it over, he looked at her face quite closely then rolled off her so they both now lay on the floor looking up at the top of the ruined castle.

"So can I do that to you for fun, if I feel it's fun?" Asked Hunter looking at her, Raine thought for a moment and then nodded. That seemed to make Hunter happy as he settled back down on the floor beside her. "What a strange place, all foggy and no colour." "I know, everything is broken, like the life has just been sucked out of it." Raine replied yarning, she did not feel tired after all the dancing, she had, had a very good night's sleep the night before, what was coming over her?

"No colour. That's. Not." That was the last word she heard from Hunter, she felt her eyes lids feel heavy, Hunter too sounded sleepy and before she could held herself she felt herself fall asleep.

For a moment she was falling, then she felt herself slow down and finally her body levelled out and she was flying. But it was dark, why was it so dark? There was nothing around her as she flew, but how could she know she was flying if it was dark?

"Hunter, where are you?" This was a very strange dream indeed, she never flew in the dark, she was always going over water or Cat's field. Then.

"Hunter!" Suddenly she was awake, there was rain falling on them, Raine opened her eyes and looked around. They were still on the floor but Hunter had cuddled up to her, how long had they been sleeping for? She wished she did not have to go home, Hunter was snuggled up to her, her arms were around him and she felt happy waking up beside him. But she had to go, it was dark, she would be in so much trouble when she got home. "HUNTER!"

"No more pants mummy." Hunter muttered before sitting upright and looking around. "Farting pants everywhere. Oh it's you Raine, it's raining, did we fall asleep?" Raine nodded and got to her feet, she looked around and wondered what had happened, why had they fallen asleep?

"Oh no." The moon was in the sky, it was still a little foggy but she could see the moon was happily playing the fiddle. "Hunter, I have to get home right away, I'm going to be in so much trouble, I don't know what they are going to say or do." Hunter seemed to understand, he took her by the hand and they ran back to the boat. Hunter rowed as fast as he could until they reached the bank of Terrae, once there he did not stop to rest. He grabbed Raine's hand and ran through Cat's field, thankfully Cat was sleeping so they did not have to stop and explain why they were running. They did not stop until they reached the green window, Poppsie was still sleeping when they got there so that saved more time. Hunter took Raine all the way to the door and waited as she fumbled with the tree to open to door to her world.

"Raine, will you come back soon so we can explore that island again?"

"Of course, I always come back to see you don't I?" Hunter nodded. Even if Louie and her Auntie's locked her away in her bedroom she knew she would run away somehow. As she smiled at Hunter she knew what she wanted to do with her grown up life. She wanted to wake up and see Hunter every morning, she wanted to have tea and cake with Jerrad and help Cat with his garden and potions.

"Ooo, I forgot to give you this, what with all the excitement of the island, dancing, falling." Hunter looked through all his pockets, then looked through all them again. "Hmm, I wonder where I put it." He looked in his side bag but clearly could not find what he was looking for. "Oh I know where it is." He said with a smile. He reached inside his coat pocket, which he had already searched twice and pulled out a green necklace. "Here, this is for you, I made it you see, for your tree. Cat used a potion to make it strong but not heavy, it the tree heavy?" He asked handing it to Raine, she shook her head and looked at the necklace. It was soft and smelt like freshly cut grass and every few links small buds of flowers sat ready to open.

"It's beautiful Hunter, thank you."

"Oh you're very welcome, Cat said it will never wilt and you never have to water it, he said it had taken to composition of metal, although I made it from flowers and grass. What's a composition then?" Raine shrugged her shoulders as she placed the tree on the chain and put it around her neck, it really was light. "Lovely, lovely. So very lovely. I will see you soon then, just like you said." Then he leaned forward and kissed her cheek, as he pulled away his while face went bright pink like bubble gum. She too felt a little shy after he kissed her cheek, it was the first time he had ever done anything like that. "Bye, bye Raine, that was a very fun day we had." He said before turning on his heels and running away. Hunter was such a strange young man, thought Raine before walking back through the door.

"But it can't be true Louie." Said Pearl looked over the pages in her hand, she felt her heart sink as Louie confirmed what was in the pages. Iris turned away and began to cry into her hands while Maud looked into her tea cup in silence. "Maybe this is just dreams, or a school project? We should ask her at least, we can't just jump to conclusions can we?"

"No Pearl, as much as we want it to be, we can't deny it, after reading this we just can't. I knew there was something going on but this." Suddenly the door opened. They each looked at one another, no one wanted to break the silence as Raine walked into the kitchen, wet from head to foot. She looked cold, wet and unusually tired.

"Oh Raine dear you are wet, come here." Pearl at once took up a dry towel from the dryer and began to patting the dear girls face. She was so dear to her, she hated to see her wet, she could catch a cold or flu.

"I'm ok, just a little wet." Then her eyes seemed to bulge from her head, they sat on the table where her diary sat. Pearl looked at it, the she looked to Iris and Maud, they did not speak as Louie got to his feet and picked up her diary. One of the many diaries they had found secretly hidden under a floor board.

"I found this in your room Raine," It was so wrong to look into the mind of a young woman, a diary was meant to be the one place she could let her secrets run free without the fear of adult eyes reading the word within. But after Louie searched her room for any sign of her location he found one diary, then he found the rest under the floor board. "Would you mind explaining what is the meaning of this."

"What do you mean, it's just a book with silly words and,"

"Stop lying." Pearl closed her eyes, she detested shouting but she detested Louie's temper even more, it was unfair how he shouted at dear Raine. She could understand his anger, his love for Raine and his desire to protect her, but he had such a temper lately. "You have described a place in here, boys, cats, strange creatures, what have you been up to Raine, tell us now or,"

"Raine dear," Iris came to her rescue, it was never Pearl's place to raise her voice, she hated to argue and detested any confrontation. "We have to know, what does all this mean, is this place. Real or in your mind?" Raine looked at the page Louie had opened in his hand. Pearl had seen many of Raine's drawings in school, but these were beautiful and so full of detail even she questioned if they were real people. The cat looked real, the man in strange bright clothes was drawn with such love and detail he had to be real.

A King sat on his throne at the head of a large table where many strange creatures joined him, and at the top Raine sat with a Cat in a wizard's hat and the same bright young man with a kind smile.

"I. I've." She sighed and took a seat at the table, she placed her head in her hand as though finally defeated. "I've been having dreams, they are so strange and real that I decided to write them down and draw them. They made very good stories you see and they made me happy whenever I felt sad. I like to read them back you see."

"Dreams? Dreams, you really think," Louie stopped as Maud placed a hand on his arm, she took the diary and closed it before turning to Pearl and Iris.

"I didn't tell you because I thought you would call me mad, in school we,"

"You know what we have to do girls?" Said Maud sadly, Pearl nodded sadly and turned away to gather her thoughts. It had to be done tonight while the rain fell, she turned to Louie and nodded her instructions, he looked at Raine and walked out of the room. "What's going on?" Her heart felt heavy as Raine looked at them all, her beautiful eyes full of confusion.

"Come on Raine we're going for a little trip." Said Iris kindly taking Raine's arm, but she shook her head and refused to get up. She was a bright girl, she knew something was not right, she knew they were doing something.

"What are you doing, why are you turning the gas on, Louie, what are you." Louie appeared with a few bags and nodded silently that everything was ready. Pearl reached inside her pocket and felt her heart sink, she never wanted this day to come and she most certainly never wanted to do this to Raine. But there was always that small chance it would come and this would happen. But now, just before she was an adult, why now, everything was so right, this place was a wonderful home to them all.

"Raine dear, have a drink before our long journey," She said looking to Louie. Before Raine could protest Louie grabbed her and secured her tightly as Pearl placed a bottle to her lips. This was horrible, she did not want to do this, but she had to.

"Let me go, let me." Raine soon stopped struggling, her eye lids fell heavy and she fell limply into Louie's arms. He picked her up and took her out to the waiting car while Pearl went to Raine's room. The old woman looked around the room, it was such a lovely room, so full of live and full of everything that was Raine. Pearl reached for a book of her drawings, some clothing and a few other items she knew was dear to Raine. After a few moments she walked out of her room and walked out of the house.

"Come Pearl, its time." As Louie checked everything was in the car and Raine was safely strapped in, the three women stood in front of their beloved little house as it slowly began to burn.

Chapter Four

Ten Years Have Passed. Alone

The night was still, silent and cold as the tree outside wrapped outside her window. She was not alone, Louie was in the same room as her tonight, he snored softly clearly in a nice deep sleep.

Raine looked at her watch and smiled, she reached for her bed covers and pulled them off revealing herself to be fully clothed.

She reached under her bed where a fully packed bag was hidden, inside were a few sets of clothes, money and food she had made before Aunt Pearl came into the kitchen. From under her pillow she pulled out a pre prepared note she had written the day before. She pulled the covers over another pillow she placed to look like herself sleeping and carefully put the note on the top.

Silently she pulled open her window and looked around, it was silent, not a single person was out this time of the night. Raine placed her bag on her back and climbed out of the window, this was easy for her, she had climbed out of the green window so many times in Ethernia so this little window was nothing.

"I wonder if," She thought sadly looking back at the small house they now lived in, but she shook that thought away as she began to quicken her pace. She had to get as far away as possible, to get a good head start before they found her gone.

Raine walked through the dimly lit town streets towards the train station, she had done this trip so many times in the past few days she could walk in with her eyes closed.

"Where to miss?" Asked the old man behind the counter, she paid for her ticket and waited the four minutes left for the train. This was train number one, she had to get a train from here to the city, then from the city to a place called Norwich and then a train back there. To that old place.

"Back home." She smiled settling down in the train carriage. She had been planning this night for what seemed like ten years, ever since that night she came back from Hunter.

It had been a blur, she lied about her diary, then her Aunts and Louie went strange, Louie forgot he was angry and packed a few things, she must have been drugged because the next thing she remembered was being in the car and far away from home. She struggled making Louie pull over, Aunt Pearl had to calm her down and tell her that they were never going back. She could not calm down, she cried the entire way and did not speak to any of them for days.

It was not until a year after Aunt Pearl told her that they had taken her away from the small town and burned the old house to the ground, she never said why. All she said was her parents had asked them to keep her safe and that was what they intended to do, it was no longer safe in that town. There was nothing in her words to say what was so dangerous in that town. "I still think it has something to do with Ethernia." She was not sure why, but something told her that it was her diary that made them run from their perfect life. Something about her words, the pictures, Ethernia must have been the reason they left.

All her belongings were gone, all but a few sets of clothes and books Aunt Pearl had taken, that and her tree, she had that with her, they never knew about that one thing. She held that tree close to her heart in the car that night, she thought about her last words to Hunter, what would he do when she did not come back?

Raine looked down in her hand and clutched the small tree and silently thanked her lucky stars they never found it. "Will you still be there I wonder, Hunter, Cat, Jerrad?" She thought sadly, it had after all been ten years since they left, ten years since she last saw Hunter and promised to see him soon.

As the train went along Raine began to think about her plan, maybe it was harsh to use sleeping pill powder in their tea. But it was the only way to ensure they would not hear her leave, she had to be sure she got a good head start. Ever since they had left their old house, someone always slept in her room, someone was always with her no matter where she went. Now she was twenty seven she felt strong enough to leave, she had saved money so she could afford the train rides and a place to stay in the town. She had planned it all in secret and felt it was water tight, nothing could stop her from going back.

She would find a job in the town, rent a small room above a shop, then they could not stop her, they could not keep her trapped in their home forever. She was now a fully grown woman and not even the four of them could stop her now.

For ten years she had lived in a new place, they had enrolled her in a new school and then a college, but she was never happy. They were always called in because she did not do her work or because she never did anything. Her Aunt's would tell the school and college that it was because of the death of her parents she was like this. But she knew they truth, her relationship with them was never the same, she never spoke to them, she just lived until one day she found her diary. Aunt Pearl had it on one of her nights, Raine picked it up and read the pages, she dreamed of Hunter, she laughed about her memories of Cat and she longed to see Jerrad again. She closed the diary after taking out a picture and that was when she started to make her plan. She looked at the train time tables, she researched the time it took to get there, the walk to the train station. Everything had to be perfect, nothing could be left to chance.

It was late afternoon before Raine reached her old village, she got off the only bus to run through and looked around. It was just as quiet and peaceful as she had left it that night. The old post office, the food market, even the fish monger was still there with the same faces working hard within.

It had been a long journey and she felt a little tired, it might be a good idea to rent a room at the Pub before going back to the site of her old home.

"It will take them a few hours to get here, that's providing they see I'm gone right away." She had made the bed looking like she was still in it and last night she had pretended she felt unwell. That was all planned of course, she had told Aunt Maud for the past few days she felt a little ill, but last night it really hit her. Her hopes were that they would leave her in bed and not disturbed her until they touched the bed clothes. "Then what a shock, but I did leave that note." At times Raine felt like a child still, leaving notes, climbing out of windows and running away was not something a fully grown woman would do. "But I had no choice, I had to, and I had to come back here." The Pub was quiet today, she was thankful for that, she did not want to see anyone who might remember her. She gave a false name in case her Aunts or Louie called ahead and told the old publican to keep her there. "I will have just a small sleep." She thought lying down on the plain bed, she held the tree in her hand and thought back to the last day she had spent in Ethernia. "I promised Hunter I would come back, Cat wanted to take me to that party and Jerrad." Raine sighed deeply and rolled over, closing her eyes as she thought about her friends. It would have been so easy if they lived in this world, she could phone or send them letters. Something. But they lived in another world, she lived in this one, and they in another.

Raine knew she was a heavy sleeper so she set an alarm to wake her in an hour, that was all she needed to refresh herself.

"So, you're a new face, haven't seen you in these parts before." Said the bar tender.

"No, I'm just here on research for a book. I'm looking for this address, I'm told the ladies there can help me." The man looked at the address on the paper and shook his head.

"No, you won't find anyone there, heck you won't even find their house anymore." Raine questioned him innocently making out she did not know what had happened. "Well, one night around ten years ago their house caught fire, five of em in that house. Three women, a man and a young girl, burned to the ground it did, fire service could do nothing to stop the fire."

"So they all died?" She asked, he shook his head and leaned on the bar as Raine finished her glass of orange juice.

"Nope, no one knows, there were no bodies to be found, all their possessions were there. Some say they died in there, some say they set the fire and left. There's a playground on their old plot, kids love it. Might be good to add to your story, another?" Raine shook her head, she thanked him for his kindness and walked out of the pub.

Ten years, how much could change in ten years, but it seemed this place did not, sure there were new faces, faces that were older than before and shops that were new. But the old school still stood in the same place, so did the bus stop Raine walked passed every morning to get to school. Even the old cat lady house still stood, but a lot cleaner with lovely rose bushes in place of the rubbish that lived there once before.

But Raine did not stop to admire the pretty town, she did not want to stop and watch the dog walkers and neither did she want to see how far the joggers could run before getting tired and leave the hilly path. She wanted to go higher, she still walked the dirt path to the old ruins, still they remained untouched, still forgotten because they were so high up.

There was her place, the hole in the ground, it was a little harder to push aside the branches and foliage, Raine thought it was due to the amount of time that had passed. Apart from climbing out of her window it had been so long since Raine had climbed anywhere. Yet, even after ten years she still found it easy to climb down the bottom of the hole. She smiled with that childlike excitement as she found her crack in the wall, she could feel herself walking faster towards the place she had visited in her dreams for the past ten years.

"It's still here." She whispered as she walked through the opening and into the room she knew so well. "I only hope." Raine reached down for her necklace, with a deep breath she took it off and placed the tree on the rock, she waited. Her heart began to fall, maybe it was not real, maybe it had all been dreams and Hunter, Cat, Jerrad and even Poppsie was not real.

But something that felt that real, that made her so happy could not have been made up in her mind, the joy and laugher she had shared with the people, and creatures in Ethernia could not have been all in her mind. Could they?

Then the tree began to glow, it was very dim, but as she began to smile brightly so did the light around the tree. "I knew it was real." The door formed, it opened for her as though it was yesterday and she walked in. Raine closed the door behind her and could not help but run, she wanted to see Poppsie, go through the green window, down the tree into the waiting Wuffle's and. "Poppsie?" Raine came to a stop and held her hands over her mouth, it was awful, she could not believe it.

Her heart was over joyed that Ethernia was real, but the hall of windows made it sink as fast as a stone in water. The windows were all broken, the wood hung off and the glass was smashed. Poppsie's chair and desk were nothing but a pile of wood and he was nowhere to be seen. "What happened here?" She said as she looked through a red window. Everywhere was grey, the blue window, the yellow, through them was void of any colour, any sound, there was no wind blowing through, nothing. "Wuffle's, where are you?" She carefully climbed down the tree for it had lost all of its leaves and most of its branches. No one came to her calls as she walked through the woods alone, Hunter was not there, the flowers were all gone. "Anyone?" She reached the edge of the woods and looked out onto Cat's field, it was dead, the grass was brown and burnt, the flowers were black dots, she wanted to turn back and go home. Something terrible must have happened here, something unspeakable had come to Ethernia and ruined it all taking all of the colour with it. "Maybe, maybe everyone is at the castle?" She thought, the quickest way to the castle was through Cat's field that she could remember. But it saddened her heart to see Cat's field so ruined, maybe it was not that fact, but the thought of what she could find. Or not find but she had to know, she had to know if everyone was at the castle or not, surely Jerrad would make the castle a safe haven for the people? Raine took a deep breath and nodded her head and began to make her way over the fallen tree and into Cat's field.

The moment she set foot on the ruined land something swept over her, she felt a wind blow her gently as she continued to walk. It pushed her like a pair of invisible hands, it tried to bare her path but she pushed one, she refused to let the wind blow her back, she had to press on and get across the field and to the castle. She closed her eyes and used her hands to shield her face from the growing wind, she had to carry on, she had to beat whatever tried to push her away. She had to get to the castle, she had to find out if Cat was safe, she had to know Hunter and Jerrad were still here, waiting for her. Then.

"Hay look, someone came through." Said one voice.

"Does Cat know?" Said a second.

"Maybe we should tell him." Said a third. Raine opened her eyes and had to double check, her eyes must be lying to her. A moment ago this field was burned and ruined, but now it was lush and green just how she had left it. she looked over her shoulder and saw the woods looked the same, but then, as her eyes looked to Cat's field her mind could not comprehend what was happening.

"I think she's a ghost girl, go tell, go tell." Said the second voice, as one of the voices left, Raine looked down to see two little gnomes looking up at her. "What are you looking at, have you never seen a gnome before you ghost girl?" It was a rather rude gnome as he crossed his arms, the second of the two nodded and stood on a rock to get a better angle to point his small finger at her.

"Yeah, ghost girl you should go away before you do any more damage." He said rudely. But what were they talking about, she was not a ghost girl, she was alive and where had they come from? Then her mind vaguely reminded her of Hunter's tales of rude gnomes.

"I'm not a ghost, I'm alive."

"A likely story." Said the first gnome.

"But it's true, you ask Cat, or Hunter, or Jerrad."

"Jerrad? You really think we're that dumb, he lived in the castle and has been dead for so long not even my grandpa remembers him." Dead? For so long? What was going on? She had only been gone ten years, how long had he been dead and what of, he was still a young man. "Go away ghost girl!"

"Yeah, go away ghost girl!"

"Claude, Mox-Mox, leave Raine alone and tend to dinner." She knew that voice, she knew right away who the cat was running towards her. "My darling, when Pooty told me here a ghost girl with crazy eyes and red hair had walked through my spell I was so over joyed, I just knew it was you, it had to be you, I just knew it." Cat was on all fours today, he held his paw up and took her hand, he rubbed his cheek against it and purred slightly.

"I'm so glad to see you Cat, you haven't changed at all." Raine could not help herself, she knew he hated to be treated like a house cat. But it had felt like a lifetime since she had seen him and she wanted to hug him like a house cat.

"Put me down Raine, I have no dignity left." He sighed as she put him back down, Cat patted himself down and began to walk. "Come, I shall take you to the safe farm, it is where they all live now, my field has become quite over crowded you know."

"But I don't know, what has,"

"It has been very busy of late," interrupted Cat shooing more Gnomes out of their way, they all pointed at Raine and stuck their tongues out or showed their bare bottoms at Cat, laughing as they went by. "Potions to make, land to tend, the Gnomes help a little you know, but not much, they think it's funny when they mess things up." What was Cat not telling her, she knew there was something he was hiding. A potion stopped people coming into the field, that much she understood and the only reason someone would do that was to protect something or someone.

"If the field has become busy, maybe something happened and here was the safest place to hide? But what could have happened?" But it was only a thought, it was a flying thought as she walked down a narrow lane, at the end was the cleanest farm she had ever seen, full of people, animals and creatures she had never seen before. There was no smell like a normal farm, there was no mess and everyone was working hard on a large table set in the middle.

"I do beg your pardon but a moment." Cat took out a potion bottle from the bag on his back and took a deep drink from it. Horses ran by and placed a table cloth over the bare table, she smiled as the Wuffle's waved at her and jumped with happiness before they bumped into one another.

"Raine!" That voice, could it really be? She felt a wave of happiness rush over her suddenly and fill her heart with a feeling she could not explain. "Raine, Raine, Raine it is you and you are real and not a ghost and not in a dream and."

"Hunter, calm down and stop squeezing so hard or she shall pop." Said Cat getting on his back legs, his fur began to change into a suit and white shirt as he walked passed Raine and Hunter. He tutted as he passed them, but Raine beamed at her smiling friend as he ran a gloved finger down her cheek.

"Oh, I don't want you to pop now you have come back. You took a very long time to come back you know, I waited by the door for days and days before I got tired and came home and then the ghosts came and,"

"Hunter!" Snapped Cat taking Raine's arm. "Don't mind him, although he has reached twenty eight, and is meant to be an adult, he is still as mad as ever. Age had not given him sanity or any maturity. But come, it is dinner time and you must eat with us." Hunter ran up to the table to picked three seats, Raine felt like she had never left Ethernia, she felt happy for the first time in ten years. She felt like she had just come home from a long trip and this was her welcome home party. Yet something was different, something was not quite right. There was something in the air, something in the eyes of Hunter as he looked at her, she knew him, she knew there was something he wanted to tell her.

"Cat," Whispered Raine. "Please, tell me what happened, what happened to the mirror's, to Poppsie, to the woods. Is Jerrad really dead?" Cat looked to Hunter, they both looked sad as the merry talking went on around them. Everyone seemed happy enough, but there was something around them, almost as if they were on edge, they all reminded her of herself the day before.

"It makes Hunter very sad to think about it." He said wiping a tear from his eyes, Cat placed his napkin down and rested his paws on the table. He sighed deeply and turned to Raine with large sad eyes.

"Many years has passed since you were last here, yes Jerrad did die darling, we all grow old and die but not those who live here like me and Hunter, he left my field so many times to check for you he aged a little every time he did." Hunter smiled and began to eat a cake as Cat continued. "No one is happy with our King now, he is not Jerrad. As to the state of the land, slowly the land lost its colour and life and as mine was the only place protected, everyone came here."

"What about you dear Raine, where did you go, what did you do, did you miss me, I mean us?" Hunter was at once full of life again as he pulled Raine's arm for attention, he was still like a child in her eyes. Raine told them how her Aunt's and Louie found her diary and took her away, she told them how she had finished school and college in another town. She told them she tried to settle down and forget Ethernia, that made Hunter a little sad but Cat explained why. He used kind words and told Hunter that it was better to forget if she was not allowed anywhere alone. She tried to get a job, but her heart was never in anything she did, she had not drawn a picture for years and her dreams had almost left her. She told them how she methodically planned her escape and how she executed it.

"A most daring escape, will they not worry about you?" Raine nodded her head and explained that they most likely knew she was back in that town and would be waiting for her when she came back.

"Do you think you will stay here, will you go back, what happens if they try and keep you away from me again?" Raine shrugged her shoulders, she had not thought beyond finding them all again and having a good long talk and catch up. What would happen when she saw Pearl, Iris, Maud and Louie?

"Oh no." Suddenly the mood changed, the food had ended and small pads began appearing in front of everyone including Raine.

"What's this?" She asked picking it up, Hunter placed his hand on the pad and stopped her from looking at it, but her curiosity over powered him. It was full of squares with people inside them, there was a girl, an old man, a group of lizards, horses, knights, all of them in their own square and all looking scared.

Everyone seemed to write something on the pad before placing it down and leaving the table looking very glum, pain etched on their faces. "Cat, Hunter, what is this?"

"It's the King, he makes us do it you know, we have no choice or he sends us to the island." That made no sense so she turned to Cat, Cat always knew the answer and Cat always made some kind of sense.

"These people are the ones who refused to choose a square or people who are brave, the King demands we choose who be sent, to Auran." He said sadly placing his paw print on the square of the lizards. "You see, anyone who goes to Auran's island never returns."

"What? So the King makes you choose people to die, that's it right, they're not going for a holiday and you all know it." Raine could not help but raise her voice, she felt so angry as she realised what Cat was trying to tell her.

"Do keep your voice down, it's very hard to even pick." But Hunter's words meant nothing to her as she picked up her own pad and turned to Cat. She knew she had no right, but she had to try, she just had to.

"I want to see this King, I want to know what's going on and why he would allow this Auran to make such an unfair demand." Cat rushed over to her and placed a paw over her mouth, he sighed deeply and pulled her over to a mushroom. He sat Raine down and rubbed his ears, this was a sure sign he was thinking.

"You do not know Auran, you do not know what he was or is. I have been around since the beginning of Ethernia and I know a lot. Believe me it had not always been so beautiful and fun like you knew and know." Said Cat rubbing his head, Hunter joined them with tea cakes and glasses of fruit water as Raine took Cat's paw.

"Then tell me, and if I still find it unfair after you tell me everything, then will you take me to the King?" Cat looked to Hunter, he said nothing and pretended not to hear as he began to eat a tea cake.

"Alright, I shall tell you, but only to make you understand and leave after your visit."

Ethernia was once bigger than four realms, they were once connected by an island with a bright castle in the centre. Parties were held for every realm and every citizen was invited, it was a place of great light, happiness and joy.

Auran was of the Firefly family, the rulers of Terrae the Realm of Earth, he was the oldest and he had two other siblings, Jerrad Firefly and Terra Firefly their youngest sister. They attended parties with their parents until the old King and Queen died of old age leaving Terra the queen of all Terrae. This only angered Auran and he revealed a deep, dark secret of his mother. A year before Terra's birth their mother had secretly met a wandering Muse from the realm of Air, they were lovers for a short time and Terra was born of their love. The King was old but had no ruling over Terra's birth as the Realm of Earth was and always had been ruled by women. Auran thought this was the one way he could gain the throne, he thought spreading the news of his sister's half breeding would make the other leaders revolt and make her renounce the throne.

But no, it was not meant to be, the leaders of the other four Realms welcomed her, the Earth and Air Queen. She later married a fellow Halfling, a Fire, Water Prince from the Realm of Fire, of course this meant the four elements lived in them and there was a chance of their child being a child of the fifth element, Life.

Auran knew that should their child be of Life, he would never see the throne of Terrae and that child would have the throne of the legendary fifth realm, Vitam which was now void of any ruler. The last of the Life blood had died many years before, but the parties were still held in the honour of Life.

Auran knew the throne to Vitam as empty, he knew he had to do something before his sister had a child. But Terra was a benevolent Queen and she knew nothing of her brother evils ways, she gave each of her brothers a region of Terrae to rule.

While the people of Jerrad's region lived happily in his love and care, Auran's fell into darkness as he read books, he read every law there was in Ethernia to try and find a way to the throne of Vitam. It was not until all his people had left his region did his sister and brother find out how power mad he had become, he had fallen so deep into madness he admitted that he had lead the attack on the island of Vitam, which had led to its demise. His troops were ghosts, the people living on the island of Vitam had been poisoned by Auran and their souls were his to command. There was nothing the siblings could do but call for the four realms to unite and seal their mad brother away on the island, leaving it a grey and misty place. The throne of Vitam would never be filled, Auran's war had seen some many die before the rulers sealed him.

Terra and her King lost their lives on the last day of the battle leaving Jerrad to rule over the land of Terrae. He never married and never took a ward to pass his title onto, but he ruled wisely and kept his part of Auran's seals safe so his mad brother could not be set free to continue his selfless war against Ethernia.

Raine looked to Hunter, he seemed to have the same look in his eyes, that island Auran was sealed on, it sounded just like the one they found when she was there last. Maybe this was all her fault. Maybe because they visited the island that made something happen and Auran was set free.

"You see, the day you left for the last time, the island began to glow in a dim light. It was a matter of days and a mist began to emit from it." Hunter began to drink from his glass deeply, Raine knew he was trying to avoid the conversation, she knew him so well. "Nothing happened while Jerrad was alive you see, I'm not sure why but the moment he died and a new King sat on the throne the mist came and we had to choose people to be sent to Auran's island."

"So, the people who get sent to Auran, they make him more powerful?" Asked Raine taking the tea cake from Hunter, Cat nodded darkly making Raine shiver. She did not want to even think about what could possibly be happening to the poor people being sent there. "The last time I was in Ethernia we went to that island, I think it's more than a coincidence that Auran came just after I left. Maybe we did something without knowing."

"What ever happened on that day I am sure it's not your fault darling, there is nothing we can do but do as the King says." Raine was almost outraged at Cat's reply, she got to her feet and took the pad in her hands.

"No, you may have to but I don't, someone should reseal him or kill him."

"Kill!" Cried Hunter getting to his feet, he dropped the last cake on the floor and let the glass fall and shatter on the ground.

"Yes, if it has to be done, one man can't rule an entire world and he most certainly can't make a world live in fear like this. I want to see this so called King." Cat and Hunter stood silently, they looked at one another as Raine stood firm and waited.

"Raine," Cat sighed deeply and got to his booted paws, he cupped his Paws and looked down before returning his eyes to her determined face. "Come with me."

The three walked through the ruined court yard, it broke Raine's heart as she remembered fondly the beautiful castle as it once was. This King clearly did not care, Jerrad always told her that the state of the castle and of the world around that castle showed the true heart of the King. That made sense now Cat explained the kingdom of Life, their land had no King or Queen so their land was gone, now used as a prison for Auran.

"Raine, Hunter, stay here, I shall get us an audience with the King." Cat was well connected, he seemed to always have the ear of the rulers.

Raine and Hunter stood in the deserted hallway leading to the Throne room, Hunter began to twiddle his finger tips and shuffle his feet. Raine looked at him, it had been so long since they had seen one another, what was he thinking, had he really went to the door and waited for her all that time?

"Hunter," She began, but the doors opened and stopped her, Cat nodded silently telling them to follow him. "I wonder what type of man this King is." Thought Raine as they walked into the Throne Room. This place too was ruined, the roof had holes, vines had taken over the walls and the lovely map had all but gone. "Clearly he doesn't care, look at the state of this once lovely room." Cat took them passed the Throne and through a small door behind, once inside Raine had to adjust her eyes, it was so dark and cramped.

"Your majesty, this is Raine." A large chair spun around revealing a little fat man in thick rimmed glasses. This was the King? This fat, dirty looking little rat of a man was given the throne after Jerrad had died, what was Ethernia thinking?

"Yes, so I hear. What do you want and make it fast, we are playing a game of strategy." He said with a slimy voice, it made her feel sick as he grinned at her. "Well, what are you waiting for, Cat tells me you want to talk to me about something or another."

"Yes, in fact I do." She replied, she decided that nice was not the way to be, she had to be strong because it was clear no one in the realm of Terrae was, no one stood up to this so called King. But today, she would. "I got your little gift,"

"Oh that's nice. What gift?" The fat King leaned over to the well-dressed man standing beside him, talking over the rim of his glasses.

"I'm talking about the pad with the boxes."

"Oh that, you must choose a box so that we may,"

"Send people to a possible death?" She began to raise her voice, this seem to surprise the little man as she did not wait for him to speak. "Do you really think by sending people to Auran as he asks that he will leave you be, have you even seen your land outside this room?"

"No, should I?"

"Yes you should you foul, poor excuse of a King!" She could not help but let her words run away with her, she felt Cat pulled on her sleeve but she took a step towards the little man as his face turned redder and redder.

"You dare speak to me like that,"

"Yes I do, your no King. What you are doing is wrong, Jerrad was more of a King to this land than you, he loved this land and took care of it, his loved showed in all corners of Terrae and you have let his love turn to ash. The castle is in ruins, the Wuffle wood is all but dead and the ones who live have to survive in one field while you sit here playing games."

"Raine," Cat placed a paw on her arm and tried to pull her back, but she was having none of it.

"You knew Jerrad, he was a good King." Said the tall man, the King shot a hot glance at him, silencing him at once, that seemed to be the only thing he could do.

"And what would you have me do, raise an army and fight Auran?"

"Go to him, talk to him you're a King of Ethernia, start acting like one. Wars are only fought because words were either not made or not spoken correctly." Replied Raine, in her many days stuck in with Louie she had used the time to read everything from the wars of swords to the battle of guns. She had a fondness for history.

"Talk she says, I do not intend to go near that island and talk to anyone thank you very much."

"Then let me!" There was a gasp from everyone in the room at her outburst, everyone, even the King was stunned at her passion. But it was not an outburst made in the moment, she would go to Auran, she would speak to him, she would do her best to talk him down, to come to some kind of agreement.

"You would go to the Misty Island and talk to this mad man, all for this Realm?" Asked the tall man, Raine turned to him and tried to show him she spoke the truth, that she was determined to help.

"Yes I would."

"Then you are a bigger fool than I thought." Laughed the King patting his large, grotesque belly as he did. Once he stopped laughing he blew his nose and wiped a small tear of laugher from his eye. "I, you do make me laugh. But it's know, and it's the law," he said with all the air of a sloth. "That only a citizen of Ethernia can approach a royal, that only a citizen of this land can approach Auran, and that is something you are not. So run along and,"

"I could marry her." Said Hunter suddenly. The room went silent again, even Raine looked to Hunter unsure what he was thinking. Was he having another one of the mad moments where he said anything to change the mood?

"Well," hummed Cat crossing his arms, a sure sign he was pondering the thought over. "If you were to marry that would make you a citizen of Terrae, it would work." He said looking to Hunter, he was no doubt impressed with this, so called good idea. "It is a very good idea, if talks did not work, she could be able to seal him away. With your blessings of course Majesty."

"Oh I bless your marriage and any type of sealing effort but I won't help you, no. No resource will be given or any helpers. My word is law and that's it."

"But they have your blessing?" Asked Cat with a large grin on his face. As the King nodded and turned back to his game Raine could not believe what was happening.

"Yes, Yes, Yes. And since one or both of you will no doubly die, I shall have no need to send people this time around. So yes, have the blessing if it means that much to you."

"I will help her of course as I am not under your rule Majesty, so I can help you Raine." Said Cat.

"Me too," smiled Hunter, it was almost as if he could not understand what he had just said, what he proposed.

"I don't care how many of your little field goes to help her, I will not help. Not now and not ever." Raine took a step up to the back of the chair, she chose her next words very carefully and hoped they hurt the foul little man.

""You are the poorest excuse of a King I have ever had the misfortune to meet. You will never be a fraction of a King Jerrad was." The Kings chair spun around and his red, fat face looked back at her with all the anger she knew would give him a bad day and game.

"Get out, get out, throw them out, never let them back in this castle again."

"Oh don't worry we're leaving, I have to plan this wedding and make it the grandest Ethernia has ever seen since Terra herself." Said Cat dancing on the spot with excitement.

"Get out, I am King, I am King, stop talking about passed rulers, I am the King." He said jumping up and down on his chair like some spoilt little brat. Raine could not help but laugh with Hunter as they left the angry little King to throw his tantrum. "Stop laughing at me." That was the last words she could hear as they walked into the Throne room.

"Oh that was the most fun thing I have seen in so many years, and I have lived many." Said Cat running his paws together like an evil villain.

"I am sorry, I didn't mean to be so rude, that's not like me at all." Said Raine now feeling rather ashamed of her behaviour. She had never been so rude and, in her mind, aggressive before, even her arguments with Louie had never been so full of anger.

"Oh no, you are very passionate, you care and it shows in your words and actions speak louder than words. And that will bring people to your wedding, oh what a fool that King is, to give you blessings without even, oh but I waste time. Let me prepare the wedding and gather support. I shall not let you down." Cat seemed more excited than she did, and clearly Hunter, as he ran out of the castle leaving Raine and Hunter in silence.

Raine looked at Hunter, he was searching the room, he shuffled his feet with his hands behind his back as she tried to guess what he was thinking. It was hard to tell if he was thinking, he had changed so much, in small ways and large since they had last met. Maybe he had grown out of many of his habits, maybe he had no more, maybe he was sane now he was older, but maybe not.

"Hunter?"

"Yes?" Such innocence, there was no sign of madness in his reply, nor was there any sanity in his face so it made her next words all the more harder.

"Do you really understand what you said in there, truly?" Hunter placed his hand on his chin and seemed to think for a moment before nodding his reply. "But. Don't you want to marry for love, to someone you love?"

"Well, I see it as," he began to show his old mad ways as he tried to explain the reasoning behind his thinking, if there was any put behind the idea of getting married. "If us getting married helps, then that's a good thing right?" Raine tried to reply but they were interrupted by the tall man from the King's room.

"Excuse me, forgive the interruption." He was very well spoken out of the King's company, he seemed old in comparison but very wise in his eyes. "My name is Dallan, I am Royal Advisor to the King."

"Well nice to meet you Dallan, have you come to throw us out?" Dallan laughed and shook his head.

"Oh no, I have no more authority than the King."

"What do you mean, he is the King right?" Asked Raine. Dallan looked behind him and ushered them out of the Throne Room. Once they were outside he walked with them through the remains of the ruined garden. Raine had such beautiful memories of this once beautiful place, now it was but a shadow of its former self.

"The King is King only in title, he is not of noble blood." That much was clear, in history books royalty had a look about them, an air of grandeur that was void from that fat little man. "I have always served in that castle, or what is left of it. I have had my thoughts for many years now, my grandmother told me of the great King Jerrad you see, it was strange how a new King was placed on the throne when he had no ward."

"So you know a lot about the royal family?" Dallan shook his head.

"No, only a few things I have heard, whispers. I do know, however that Jerrad was the middle child, that Queen Terra handed him the throne in her Will because she knew he would rule in her light. He was a very kind man, it is strange you should know him personally." It was not strange now Cat explained about his field, time never moved in that place and so Cat never aged. "Yes, and Cat did tell the King you were from another world, that your name would be in the royal records. I doubt he will ever read them and he keeps them locked away for some reason or another."

"Cat already explained the history of the Firefly family, its rather sad a war started between a family because one became mad with power." Hunter agreed with Raine as they reached the dried fountain, she sat on the edge and looked at where the once clear waters fell. She had many happy conversations with Jerrad about everything and nothing here. He had told her how Terra was an old world meaning earth and that all the realms followed the same. He had promised, when she was old enough, he would take her to visit the other lands. She had, of course asked if Hunter could join them, Jerrad had laughed and said he may. He also said how they were joint at the hip, that everywhere she went, Hunter would follow, he wished to have such a someone that would follow him where ever he went.

"Yes, but it was a great time of unity for Ethernia," Dallan interrupted her memories suddenly.

"Unity?"

"Yes Raine, unity. You see, the other four realms live in the same land, but live separate lives, they do cross over at times, yes, but live sprite lives. Once Terra sent word of her brothers intent they held a meeting, it was only a matter of words and the confirmation that he had destroyed Vitam did they all decide to unite and seal him in that place. I do know of the other realms, would you like to hear?" Hunter looked at Raine, eager for all the history she could gather Raine nodded, feeling like she was in school again. "Then I shall tell you of the three realms, no doubt Cat has told you more than you need to know of this."

The realm of Air, A'ris sits high on a cloud in the north or Ethernia. They were and always have been a peaceful race full of teachers, scholars and the gifted in the mind. They detested all forms of noise and often live in pure silence. The rulers are of pure decent, they have never invited blood of another realm though it has been known for the citizens to leave and never return as they unite with others from different realms. The people of A'ris are the teachers of Ethernia, they open their doors to those in need of knowledge and always play host to chess tournaments once a year during the time of the brain.

Naturally it is always they who win and normally the people of Ignis take the loss very badly and often start fires. Ignis is quite the opposite to A'ris, they are a people of noise, fighting and fire. Their realm is divided up into villages with one main village in the centre where the royal Chief and wives live. They too have their own festivals, though many do not venture to them as they always end up in some kind of fight or burning of the trousers. They are not as bright as the other realms, in fact they are very primal and caveman like in their appearance, to wear the skin of your largest kill is a great honour for any man of Ignis.

Finally the realm of water, Aqua, lies at the bottom of the sea, their entire realm lives under waves of glorious blue and they very rarely have visitors. They are of fish decent and many have fins and tails to help with their day to day lives. They live for words, no one ever writes anything down and so many a great song or poem has been lost, for the people of Aqua always talk in rhyme and song.

All four Realms, Terrae, A'ris, Ignis and Aqua centred around one island, Vitam, the realm of Life was the centre of life, of the entire world of Ethernia until Auran destroyed it.

"Wow," Sighed Raine, she liked the sound of the other realms, the different people, she found ii fascinating how each race had the characteristics of their realm. She wondered if she would ever see the rest of Ethernia like Jerrad had promised.

"Each realm has its laws on the King or Queen, so you see, Terrae was meant to be led by a Queen and her King, that is why I suspect the King is not noble blood and that fact is why Auran was bitter and vengeful."

"Well, to be over looked as the oldest for the throne would make anyone angry," said Raine getting to her feet, the stone was making her bottom cold. "But not to this extent, its rather mad."

"Like me?" Asked Hunter with a bright smile.

"Hunter, no matter how mad anyone claims to be they can never beat you." This reply seemed to please Hunter.

"Yes, this brings me to the last reason I wished to speak to you both, do you really intend to marry for the sake of our land?" Asked Dallan clutching his old hands together, but Raine was not given the chance to reply as Hunter jumped to his feet.

"Yes, of course."

"Then, I wish to offer my services to marry you both. I have always dreamed of performing a royal wedding but alas I fear there will be none. But a union for the sake and aid of an entire land would outweigh the honour." That again, Raine had nearly forgotten about Hunter's mad idea to get married, she was not sure if it was the best idea. Yet, as

Hunter pointed out, if it mean they could help and seal Auran away, maybe it was for the best.

"That's, I, it is a very lovely offer. I just." Raine closed her eyes and held the tree in her hand, she needed to think, this was just all so sudden. She had never pictured getting married, she had never thought there would be a chance. She thought she would die an old lady with her Aunt's, or maybe she would marry Louie, maybe she would never marry. "I need to go and think, excuse me." She walked away from Hunter and Dallan and placed her hands in her pockets. She needed to stop holding the tree, Jerrad was no longer there to ask for help. "He would most likely have laughed and said Hunter was mad. But then again he would never have let this happen." She sighed deeply deciding where to go.

She would go to Wuffle wood, there she knew she could be alone for a while to think. As she walked she felt a slight chill, she walked around Cat's field taking the long route to the woods. She did not want to pass Cat, he would be making preparations for her wedding, no questions asked and she did not want to see that just yet. She had to think about this logically.

Once there she found a fallen tree and sat down, could she marry Hunter, she knew him very well and they did get along, they were joint at the hip said Jerrad. They were two peas in a pod said Poppsie. Friends linked forever, her own words of course.

But she wanted to marry for love, she wanted to marry someone who would love her forever, someone she knew who cared for her and someone she could grow old with. She understood what it meant to marry, to be bound for life in wedlock, but did Hunter. He did not seem to understand anything, he chased Pompom's for most of his life thinking they were real creatures. Maybe this was not the right thing to do, she could just leave, forget Ethernia and Auran. After all, it was not her land, nor her problem.

"Raine Darling?"

"Cat," Raine turned around and smiled at Cat as he walked over on all fours, his potion had worn off as he was back to wearing his own fur. He was still a fine sight without his suit, but in her eyes a cute, fluffy house cat she wanted to pet and hug.

"I thought I would find you here, Hunter said you were off thinking about something or another, he didn't catch on why you left though, he's not too smart in that department and reading was never his forte." Raine smiled. "Here put this on, it is very cold these days out side of my field."

"This is Hunter's." Said Raine putting on Hunter's favourite coat, Cat smiled and nodded as he helped her put it on. It was still very warm.

"Yes, he told me to give it to you, he said you might be cold and sneezels could never do for a wedding." Cat climbed onto the fallen tree and sat beside Raine, he held his paws on his lap and let his little legs dangle. "Raine, I know what you are trying to think about." Did he, did he really know? "Hunter may be as mad as a fruit cake, but he is and always has been a good person, now a man. He would never let any harm come to you, why do you think he always walked you to the door?" He did always walk with her, her teenage mind had never thought of it further than him being polite. "Personally, I believe you shall both help the land, together." Cat place a bow and a set of arrows on the ground in front of her and jumped off of the tree and began to walk away. "I know it's not what your used to, but you're a grown up and you don't play with toys anymore." He said over his shoulder. Raine looked over hers and watched as Cat wandered out of sight. She looked back to the bow and arrows and sighed deeply, she knew what Cat told her was true. She was terribly fond of Hunter, she cared about him so much, but enough to get married?

She was not sure, maybe it was time for her to go home and forget Ethernia, after all, as Cat said, she was grown up now and grownups do not play.

Chapter Five

The Lost Raine

"Hunter's getting married."

"Hunter likes a girl."

"Hunter and the ghost girl sitting in a tree, K.I.S.S.I.N.G!"

"Oh, tea." Hunter ran over to Cat's table and poured himself a cup of tea, he liked tea. He did like fruity things more, but he did like tea. Where was Cat anyway, he had seen him, given him a coat to give to Raine, because going for walk was a very cold thing to do and that was it.

"Hunter's been kissing!"

"I wonder where Cat could have gotten to, oh well, more tea for me." He smiled and walked up to his tree house, he was so very happy that he did not have to share it with anyone, they all had their own tents to live in. "I could always make room for Raine if she wants to stay after our adventure." He thought looking up at his small tree house. He would have to build more to it, it was a rather small tree house now even for him. Maybe he would make Raine a room all of her own, full of girl things, whatever girl things were. Cat could help there, he was so smart.

"I hope you're not drinking all of my tea again, you are worse than that horse eating my acorns." Cat was back from his walk, Hunter turned around and hid the tea cup behind his back. "Why did you let Raine go off on her own?" Asked Cat smacking Hunter's knee, he dropped the cup making Cat shake his head as he begun to clean it up.

"She wanted to go for a walk, so I let her, she likes walking."

"I know that, but don't you want to talk to her about it?" Hunter wondered what Cat was talking about, why should they want to talk about a walk? You walked on a walk, he thought that was clear even to him, you go for a walk to walk and some people liked to walk alone while others like to walk with people. "I mean about the wedding."

"Oh, that, she's off walking about it, she's fine." Cat sighed and took Hunter's hand, he sat down with Cat and wondered what was going on, was he in trouble again for breaking another tea cup?

"Hunter, you need to understand, getting married is not a game."

"I know, my mum and dad were married you know and they told me all about it, it does sound rather fun you know, why are you not married

Cat?"

"It's not fun to Raine!" Snapped Cat suddenly, he had never spoken to him like that before. Cat never once raised his voice or snapped at him, not even when he was angry at him.

Cat had looked after Hunter since he was a child, he could not quite remember his parents fully and he could not remember why they were not here. Maybe they did not tell him all about getting married, maybe Cat or Jerrad did. "I think Raine is confused, she might leave Ethernia." Leave, but why, they were going to get married and go on an adventure to seal Auran away so the colours came back and everyone could move away from the field. He would like everyone to go back to their home now, it was a little boring for him. But now Raine was back, they could go out together again like they used to as children. "No Hunter, what you need to understand about Raine, or most females for that matter, they want to marry for love. They have a romantic idea about marriage you know. It came as a shock to just hear you say, let's get married like that. It was like saying, lets got for a walk or a swim."

"Raine can swim, I taught her."

"Please keep your mind on this Hunter, you need to understand it's not a game, it's something that can and will change your paths, it will unite them, you will walk the same path once you unite in heart and soul. Do you understand that, you will be united for life." Hunter sat back and took his hands away from Cat's warm paws. He got to his feet and began to walk away. "Hunter, what are you doing?" He turned around and looked down sadly.

"I do know, and I understand, just because I don't seem very smart doesn't mean I'm not smart at all, I know it's not a game." He said. Cat looked down, he began to purr loudly as Hunter walked away from the wind mill land towards the Wuffle woods.

It had been a very long time since he had left Cat's field, when Raine had left he went back so many times to wait for her, he even fell asleep a few times waiting. But she never came back, he thought she might be very busy with the thing called school. But still he waited in hope she would come back, but now she was back, now she was here and wanting to help he was not so sure what to do now.

Hunter looked up as he nearly fell over a fallen tree, there she was, she was firing a bow thingie Cat never let him touch. She was still very good at shooting, he was happy she had not forgotten their games with the Floober thingie. He had lost that when the ghosts came.

"Hunter, you startled me."

"Well, you have to be silent if you want to catch Pompom's you know, have you seen any since you came back?" Raine looked down and smiled with a shake of her head. She had very nice hair colour, it was still red like fire burning brightly. Raine walked to the bank of the lake and looked over at the foggy filled island, what was she thinking that made her look so sad?

"Maybe I will ask." He thought walking up to the bank, there was still that fog, it was very thick now and very scary looking.

"It's so sad," She said suddenly. "The world was so beautiful when I left, now, well now it looks like that island over there."

"Well, Cat did protect us in the field you know, it still has a lot of colour, so it's not all that bad Raine."

"Do you think it's my fault?" What? "I did go to the island with you, everything was fine until I went there." She placed her chin in her hands and sighed very loudly and very sadly. It made Hunter fell very sad when she sighed like that, and it made him want to cry to see her sad like that. "Do you think I was wrong to write about this place, for even coming here in the first place?" Hunter may have been mad, but even a mad man in his wrong mind knew sense.

"Raine," He knelt in front of Raine and took her nice warm hands in his. "Do you remember when you first come here, when we first met?" Raine looked like she was going to cry as she smiled a little and nodded. That made him happy, she did remember. "So do I."

"Happy birthday to you, happy birthday to you, happy birthday dear Raine," it was her birthday, Raine was very excited because now she was six years old. Louie had got her a nice book to draw things in while Auntie Maud made her a cake, Auntie Pearl got her colourful pens to use and Auntie Iris made her a scarf.

"Can I go out and play. Please?" She asked with a large smile, she had been so very good today and it was her birthday. But her Aunties never let her go out, they said no and that she must go and get ready for her party. Raine did not want a party, the other children did not like her, they only wanted to come because their parents bought them.

"Silly old party." Said Raine sitting down on her bed, she picked up her scarf and put it on, it was a very nice scarf with blue, green, red, yellow and white stripes on it. "Maybe I could sneak away like a mouse and they won't notice that I've gone away?" She thought that would be lots of fun, she had always wanted to go and see where the dogs went for a walk.

Raine picked up her coat and sneaked downstairs, her Aunties and Louie were all in the kitchen getting ready for the party in the garden.

Raine smiled to herself and thought she was so very clever for sneaking out like that, she ran down the path and through the village.

When she saw a man walking with his dog she followed him, they walked up a path to the hills. She was very glad to have bought her coat and scarf because the higher she got the colder it became. "Wow, what a pretty castle." She cried running up to what looked like a broken castle. What a lovely birthday this was turning out to be, a castle just for her to play in. Raine ran through the rocks and climbed up before jumping off again, sometimes falling and scrapping her knees.

"Oh look, it's her, the small funny looking girl." Raine stopped playing and turned around, three bigger boys that was in her class ran up to her. They were not very nice at all, they pushed her around making her fall over.

"It's my birthday, please leave me alone."

"Oh, I never knew it was your birthday," said the biggest boy, he held his hand out ready to help her get to her feet again. "Let's give you the bumps!" He cried, but Raine pulled her arm, they were so mean to her.

"Stop wriggling squirt or you'll fall." Said another boy.

"Fine." The biggest boy pushed Raine, but the floor was not there, she felt like she was falling for a long time before she felt herself hit the hard ground and roll a few times. "Oi, squirt, are you there?" She could hear them but it was a little dark, she had fallen down a hole.

"What's that, hay squirt!" There was a rumble and stone started to fall down, Raine looked around and saw a tunnel, she ran down at as she heard thunder rumbling behind her.

Raine coughed a little, there was so much dust everywhere, she looked back and saw that way was all covered up with rocks.

"Am I stuck?" She thought, with that she sat down and began to cry, what a terrible birthday, now she would be lost forever because she did not tell anyone where she was going. Suddenly her sobs was joined with small laugher, Raine stopped crying and looked around, there was a door in the rocks and a hole and an eye looking through. "Hello eye." She said walked up to the door, again the eye laughed but this time the door opened. Raine walked in and looked around, this was a room of rocks, the door suddenly closed behind her and a boy ran passed her. "Hay, hay you come back." She called as she started to run after the boy. He was so fast, he laughed as she chased him, it was getting to be fun as she followed him down a very long hallway until they reached a big open room.

Raine stopped to see where the boy had gone, there were windows all of different colours, there was one green one left open. Suddenly a man grunted, making Raine very scared, he looked so big and round, so she ran to the window and pulled herself up and through it.

Raine then began to scream as she began to slide very fast down something, then she landed in something that moved with long arms. But she saw the boy waiting for her, he ran away again laughing as he did and Raine was soon up and chasing him again. She felt like she was inside a book she once read with auntie Pearl. "Hay come back, you're too fast!" She called as the boy ran through a field, he stopped at a bridge and let her catch up, before running over the bridge. "Hay, I can't run, help!" As she stopped halfway over the bridge she heard a crack, and she fell into the water. Raine began to panic, she could not swim, she flapped her arms but that only made the water splash in her face, but that only made her feel more scared.

Then she felt her head come out of the water, someone held onto her very tightly and took her out of the water. Raine lay down on hard ground again and breathed very deeply, she was very scared her heart was going boom, boom, boom.

"Are you ok?" Raine opened her eyes to see who the voice was, she sat up and looked at the boy who had run away from her.

"I'm ok now, did you save me?" The boy nodded with a large smile and began shaking the water from his head. "Hay," the water drops went all over Raine.

"My goodness, are you children alright?" Raine could not be awake, maybe she was asleep because a cat was running over to them, he stood up once he reached them and began patting her face with his paws. "Oh you poor dear, you are wet, wet, wet. Hunter, why did you take her swimming, you know all new people must come to the King." The cat turned back to Raine, who did not know there was a king or who the Hunter was. "My name is Cat, this is my field and that, well that is Hunter, he is a little crazy sometimes. Come on, let's get you dried off and see if I can't make some fruit drinks."

"Yeah, fruit drinks!" Cried the boy as he jumped to his feet and ran away, he liked to run a lot, maybe when they were all dried off they could run again. This time without any falling into water.

"I remember me and Cat came back to the Windmill and there you was, holding a broken cup in one hand and a banana in the other." Laughed Raine and Hunter as they remembered her first visit. It had been a magical day, Cat had used a potion to dry her off and made them all a nice tea. She told them who she was and that today was her birthday. Cat and Hunter gave her a lovely birthday cake and took her to see Jerrad, he was very pleased to meet her. He gave her the tree and told her that once Hunter took her to that door all she had to do was place the tree on the same rock and she could come back whenever she wanted.

"I also was surprised you couldn't swim, so I said if you come back I would teach you to swim so you didn't fall into water again."

"And you did teach me to swim, and climb really good, we had fun days." Smiled Raine fondly remembering, Hunter smiled as he sat beside her, he held one of her hands in his own and squeezed it tightly.

"Raine," that was a very serious way of calling her name, even for Hunter. "You do know it's not your fault Auran came back and you don't really have to stay and help." Raine looked down, she knew that, deep inside she knew it was not her fault, people can't stay sealed away forever.

"I want to help Hunter, this place feels like home for me, it has and always will be a special place full of special people I care about."

"Even me?" Asked Hunter shyly.

"Yes, even you." Smiled Rain rubbing his cheek with the back of her fingers. Hunter smiled again and leaned forward and kissed her lips so suddenly and quickly she was taken back. That was something she had not expected from Hunter, a kiss on the lips, he shyly looked back at her.

"Cat said some things to me you know, I want you to know it's not a game to me, and I may not be that smart you know but I do try and be good, even though I'm a little mad." Raine knew he was a good man, from the day they met as small children she knew he was a good person, even though he was mad. "So," Hunter got off the fallen tree and knelt in from of her taking both of hands in his with a new brightness in his eyes. "I know we are marrying for a different reason, but Raine, will you be my wife and marry me in union?"

"Hunter," Raine was lost for words, this was the most adult, sane thing she had ever heard him say, it was also the most romantic thing anyone had ever said to her. But he knelt there waiting for her to reply, and she could not leave him waiting there forever. "Yes I will Hunter."

"Really? Yeah!" Hunter pulled Raine to her feet and began to spin her around until she felt quite dizzy. "Oh that's dizziness." He said holding his head slightly, but with a smile he turned to her and gave her a big hug. Raine had never been held like this before, she placed her head on his shoulder and closed her eyes for a moment. She felt very safe there in his arms. "Raine," Hunter pulled her back and looked in her eyes with a soft shy smile. "Can I kiss you? For real, not a wedding kiss, but a real kiss?" Raine smiled shyly and nodded. She had never kissed anyone before, she had never really thought about kissing anyone like this. She felt warm, she really liked kissing Hunter.

The field was bubbling with talk of the wedding, Raine and Hunter walked through the preparations hand in hand happily. Hunter told her all about his idea for his tree house and how he wanted to help make the Wuffle wood all better again.

"Cat said he was trying to make a potion to help, but he's not been able to you know." It was so nice to be able to talk to Hunter like this, she almost forgot why they were getting married. But as they walked towards Cat's windmill she saw Dallan and she remembered. But Cat and Dallan was not alone, there was a girl standing with them.

"Hunter, Raine, there you are, I was beginning to worry." Smiled Cat walking over to them.

"No, there's nothing to worry about Cat." Smiled Raine looking to Hunter, he squeezed her hand and smiled in return.

"You are Raine, yes you are just as he described." The girl walked over to them and held her hand out. "Please forgive me, my name is Talia, I am the sister of the King." Raine became confused as Talia bowed in her direction, surely it should be the other way around.

"Once I informed Lady Talia of your wedding and who you were, she at once wished to meet you." Explained Dallan joining them.

"Yes, you see, I found the works of King Jerrad, many of the papers were lost and we have yet to read through them all, I have asked Dallan here, once the Sealing of Auran is complete to aid me. But I digress." She was very sweet, her voice almost sang her words in a song. "Jerrad spoke of you in the passages I have read, he spoke of your first visit, how he invited you to come whenever you pleased. He also explained how time worked for us and for you, but it is of no importance. Dallan has told me his thoughts on my brother and it is time the truth be known." Cat ushered them toward his table and continued writing as they sat and spoke.

"What truth do you mean?" Asked Raine, she was surprised to see that Talia was completely different to her brother. She was. Nice.

"We are not of noble blood," So Dallan's thoughts were correct, the King had no right sitting on that throne. But she did not fully understand, how did he become King? "You see, each Realm has their own royal seal, this is an item that shows their royal blood line, their right to the realm, if you please. Jerrad, as you know was handed the throne by Terra but had no children, no ward and when he died, his seal disappeared with him. Now I am unclear as to how, but my great-grandfather cheated his way to the throne, and my family has been there ever since." Talia had really done her homework, she knew her stuff, thought Raine as she took all the information in and put it all together.

"You see it is my belief that,"

"My lady, please forgive my interruption." Dallan took a step forward, he was very polite in his interruptions if nothing else. "But if the Union is to go ahead we must complete the tasks at hand."

"Tasks?"

"Yes Raine, to marry Hunter and seal Auran you must first have the blessing of the other three realms and gain their seals." Explained Talia sitting forward, so Talia was on their side, she wanted to defy her brother and help Terrae. "To seal Auran requires a ritual and you need the four royal seals in order to complete it, I have read this thoroughly but the passage on Life contribution is missing. But my feeling is that will become clear as we travel Ethernia."

"Travel, you mean we're leaving Terrae?"

"Why yes, in your many visits have you never left?" Raine shook her head and got to her feet with excitement. "Then we have not a moment to loose, I shall accompany you, for my title shall grant us an audience with the rulers. But I am afraid once there is shall be down to you Raine to convince them to part with their seal and grant their blessing."

"That will be easy, just look they are lovely. I shall come too, the residents can complete the rest of the ceremony. And Dallan said he will finish the rest of the papers, of course your coming too Hunter?" Asked Cat, Hunter nodded with excitement and ran to his tree house, everything was happening so fast Raine could hardly keep up with everything. Ethernia moved so fast compared to her world and she felt a little lost as everyone began to prepare for the journey.

"So, where are we going first?" Raine stood with Talia, she looked at a map from her pocket and began to mutter to herself.

"I think it will be better if we go to the Window's and go through to A'ris, I had Cat check them before Hunter left to find you. It is the only window left, after that I suggest we go to Ignis and then Aqua. Since the city of Aqua is quite close to Vitam it should be no problem locating a Turtle to take us back here. Then you shall marry and we may seal Auran." Talia placed the map back in her pocket and turned to Raine. She was a very sweet looking girl, she wondered why the fat little King was given the throne and not her, clearly she was better suited. "Are you sure you wish to do this, for us?" Raine looked at Hunter, she smiled and returned to Talia and nodded her reply, there was no words left to say between anyone. Cat gave Raine a small bag full of things she would need, and then hand in hand with Hunter they walked towards Wuffle wood and her first visit to another realm. A'ris.

Chapter Six

The Realm's of Ethernia

"It will not be hard to gain an audience with the King of A'ris," Said Talia as they all walked onto a waiting cloud. "I have visited him many times before, he shall surprise you I am sure."

"You know," said Raine taking a seat beside her. "You're so much more, how can I put this without insulting your family? Better than your brother." Talia laughed behind her hand regally with such grace it was easy to see that she should be a princess not only in title.

"I thank you for the kind words, but we are only half related. You see, my mother was royal advisor to the realm of Air, I was born to her while she was married to her young lover. But he sadly died young and she was given to the King of Terrae and they had him." It sounded very much like Talia did not care much for her brother either, she had yet to say his name and not once spoke highly of him.

"To be honest, I have never liked your family and to hear they cheated to gain the throne, and I am even more outraged that they did not keep to the female rulers. Um, rule." Cat sat with his legs crossed while reading a book called 'Union's' while Hunter looked over the edge of the traveling cloud.

"Well, to be honest, I am glad I am only married into that family and not blood tied."

"Blood tied?" Asked Raine, more words from Ethernia she would have to lean if she were to carry on visiting.

"Oh, blood tied is to be brethren, family. In Ethernia when you are bound by blood or Union you are forever tied together unless the Union is broken by death. That is why Unions are so very important to consider before you go ahead." Explained Talia, she was very wise about most things it seemed, maybe she would make a lovely queen, or royal advisor.

"Oh, that's really nice, you see in my land you can easily cut off your family, loose them and divorce, which means to separate. I guess it would be breaking a union because you did not want to be with that person anymore." Talia nodded her head wisely and took in all the information, Raine thought she would very much like to stay friends with Talia, she was very interesting and wise for her youthful appearance.

"Arr, we are here, please, let me go ahead and announce you and your reason for visiting, although I did send word ahead." That was very resourceful of her, Raine had not thought to do that, maybe they should have done it for the other realms.

"No, it would take too long to get word to Aqua and Ignis would tear it up." Explained Cat as they walked into the great hall of the A'ris castle.

Raine was pleasantly surprised, she had expected this realm to be affected by Auran's fog too, but it was clear. The castle was made of clouds that emitted a faint glow of yellow like a buttercup, there was a soft wind blowing from the very walls. The only thing Raine found strange was how quite it was, apart from the wind there was silence surrounding them. The castle and outside reminded her of one big library.

"Please, if the party from Terrae would like to follow me." This must be the King's advisor or something close to it, he too, like Dallan had an official look about his appearance. On the back of his cloak there was a symbol.

"Cat, what does that symbol mean, I've seen it around the castle." Asked Raine in a low whisper, Cat looked up from his book and turned to the cloak, he hummed for a moment before replying.

"Did Jerrad not tell you, each Realm has its own symbol, a yellow circle with the curls belongs to the realm of air. You see, the curls represent the air blowing. Water realm has a droplet coloured blue and the people of the realm of fire have cleverly decided to have a ball of fire coloured red. As you can see a lot of thought went into it." Raine laughed, she did not want to point out that the water realm too had a simple symbol, a droplet of water.

"And Terrae?"

"A leaf." Piped up Hunter. "We have a leaf, Jerrad told me once that a rock or clod of earth was not distinguished enough so his ancestors decided on a leaf."

"Oh I see, does the Life realm have a symbol?" Cat shook his head as they walked into the throne room. There inside waiting for them was a young man, merrily talking with Talia.

"Here they are, King Foog this is Cat and Hunter of Terrae," Cat took a graceful bow before hitting Hunter in the leg to do the same. "And this, this is Raine, the young lady I spoke of." King Foog took a step forward and held his hand out, Raine took his hand and wondered if she should bow as he placed his free hand on top of hers.

"Raine, it is a pleasure to meet you, Talia has told me in a letter what you intend to do not only for Terrae but for us all." Everyone? "Auran will not stop at Terrae, he will come here, it is only a matter of time. In order the claim the throne of Vitam he must first conquer or gain the blessing of the other four." So he had already taken Terrae, who was next? It made a little more sense to Raine as she put everything into perspective, Auran had taken Terrae but must be too weak to move from the island, so Terrae sends him people and that must make him strong. At least that was her idea, and it made sense to her at least.

"Foog and myself have been meeting and corresponding on this matter for some time now, we have been decided how best to protect the other realms from Auran's advances." Foog and Talia were resourceful, they were true leaders, Raine could not help but admire them.

"From our combined knowledge we understand that our seals can grant Auran Vitam and seal him, I have my own of course here." Foog held out a glowing cloud showing them before returning it to his robes for safety.

"The only problem is I have not been able to locate Jerrad's, it disappeared."

"So you have not been able to locate it as of late?" Talia shook her head.

"It would help if I knew what I was looking for, not once in Jerrad's papers has he mentioned his seal, what it looks like, nothing. As I informed you in my last letter, he mentioned Raine, how she was a ray of light and how much she reminded him of his dear sister." That was very nice of him to say, but Raine could not remember Jerrad ever saying that to her. He always spoke of his sister with such love and affection but never really told her much else.

"Then maybe he wanted Raine to rule after his death?" There was a hint of hope in Foog's eyes as he looked to Raine, but she shook her head watching the hope fade away. She felt a little bad for taking it away so easily.

"No, Raine's world works differently in time you see, it goes slower than us I think. In her world it was but ten years since she last came, whereas here, many more." Said Cat, he was unnaturally quiet, his little nose was stuck in that book of his. What ever could he be reading that was more important than taking part in this conversation?

"I see, that is a shame. If Talia here was never to be made queen, then someone with intentions as yours should be on that throne. What I would not give to have seen Terrae in its former glory." Foog sat on his throne and placed his chin sadly on his hand. There was a sudden drop in levels in the throne room, Raine could feel the sadness sweeping passed her around each of them.

"But you can," she cried with a smile, she had to bring hope back to

Foog's eyes, she had to make them all realise that what they were doing would work. If no one believed in their plan, then it might not work. After all, if history had taught her anything, it was to believe in the cause for the good reasons. "The realm of Earth will return to the beautiful land I knew, maybe even more so. That's why I'm here, that's why Hunter and I are going to get married and seal Auran away. And to make sure A'ris doesn't suffer the same fate." Raine walked up to Foog and knelt before him. "King Foog, I ask for your blessing as King of A'ris, the realm of Air and for your royal seal so I may use it to seal Auran away forever." Foog looked down at her, his eyes suddenly gave nothing away, they studied her, scanned her, but she waited, she looked back with determination and resolve. He had to say yes, he just had to say yes.

"It would be my honour to bless your Union," Foog got to his feet and placed his hand on Raine's shoulder with a smile. "And I give you all the hope I can in your efforts to seal Auran, here my seal."

"What, just like that?" Asked Cat so full of surprise his glasses nearly fell off of his nose.

"Yes," smiled Foog handing Raine his royal seal, she smiled and looked to Talia who returned her smile. "We are a peaceful people, we do not intend to fight Auran. Unfortunately it is our nature to follow the winds of change and if Auran were to come to power and over throw me, then I have to accept it. Very much like the people of Water realm you shall see, they too flow like their water. Go, you have a long journey to get to Ignis and they are in the middle of some festival, so it might not be so easy to going their attention let alone their seal and blessing."

"Another, they do not tire of festivals?" Foog shook his head and placed a kiss on Talia hand leaving Raine to wonder if the little King secretly had feelings for the wise princess. They would make a lovely couple in her eyes, they worked so well together.

"Go now, swiftly. My cloud shall take you above the village to the King of Ignis, it is the least I can do, but tell no one I did that ok." Raine nodded and followed Talia, Cat and Hunter as they began to leave. "Good luck. In everything." Hunter waved as the doors closed leaving Foog alone in the throne room, alone with his silence and wind. Raine wondered if she could live here in A'ris, but no, the silence would be too much for her. She liked to run, scream, make sound and that would never do in a library. And she was sure Hunter would not like the silence either.

"I wish we could have stayed longer." Raine felt she would have loved to explore place, it was so quiet, so peaceful, but to live here? No, she could never do that. True to his word the cloud sat waiting for them at the walls of the palace, inside they each took a seat but this time no one said a word.

The cloud floated out of the city walls leaving the silent city behind as it gathered speed, Raine bid the city farewell and hoped she could see it again one day. Maybe she would play chess with someone, she was rather good at chess, Aunt Maud taught her every night it was her turn to sleep in her room and she had a fondness for it.

"I will take you there. After." Whispered Hunter, she turned to him and smiled as he took her hand and placed it on his lap. He returned his gaze to the sky and began to hum to himself once more, he was so funny, serious one moment and mad the next.

After what seemed liked hours the cloud came to a sudden stop, Raine looked over the edge and saw that they were over a rough, red hot looking terrain. She sat up and turned to Cat, he was still nose deep in his book, occasionally using his paw to push his glasses up his nose.

"We are here." Talia sounded a little apprehensive, that means she was hesitating you see, and as Raine looked over the edge again and saw rivers of fire and balls jumping from the ground she could understand why.

"Ignis?" She asked, Talia replied with only a nod. The cloud itself shivered and turned them out by turning itself upside down. Suddenly Raine felt herself falling through the air at a fast pace, she screamed as the wind blew passed her. As she looked around she saw Talia was waving her hands around while Cat still sat in the same position, still nose buried deep in his book, clearly unaware of what was happening.

"Raine." Why was Hunter smiling at a time like this, they were falling to their death because of a scared cloud and he was smiling. At least he reached out for her hand, he then turned and pulled Raine closer so he was in his arms. If she was going to die, at least she was in Hunter's arms. "Cat! Cat!" He cried over the roaring wind.

"Oh, oh yes I quite forgot Hunter." Cat pulled his glasses from his nose and slowly closed his book, he then reached inside his coat pocket and pulled a bottle out. "Here." Here opened the bottle and poured out a purple cloud.

"What is happening?" Cried Talia reaching out for Cat's outstretched paw.

"You will see." Cat's cloud became big, it flew down below them, as Raine looked down she saw the rocky land was so close she could see the people of the village looking back at her. She closed her eyes and buried her face deep in Hunter's coat.

"WEEEE!" Hunter tapped Raine shoulder as she felt herself bounce on something soft, she bounced again. And again. As she opened her eyes she saw they were bouncing on the purple cloud like some kind of bouncy castle. "It's Cat bouncy cloudy potion for falling off of thingies." Said Hunter still enjoying himself as he bounced on his head, and then his bottom. Raine stopped herself from bouncing and crawled over to the side of the cloud and helped herself off.

"I made it because he was forever falling out of his tree house." Said Cat with a deep sigh.

"I hope we didn't scare them too much." Raine helped Talia off of the cloud and looked around the village. It was very silent, still apart from the roaring fire in the centre of the village. Every hut had a red stick roof, they all had fire on the doors. The people looked at them with confusion, but no one came forward, no one spoke as Cat, Raine and Talia stood before them. Hunter on the other hand was the only one to be making any kind of noise as he continued to bounce on the cloud. "Umm, hello." Said Raine unsure of herself, she took a step forward and waved slightly. Everyone started to look at their partner, they were very odd looking, almost caveman like in her mind. They all wore some kind of animal print as their clothing, some of the men wore bones through their noses and the woman all had some kind of trinket around their necks. But Raine noticed that all of them had fire red hair, every single one of them.

"HELLOOOOOO!" One man cried.

"HELLOOOOO!" Cried his partner waving his club above his head.

"HELLOOOOO!" What had Raine done, everyone was now running around the fire shouting 'hello' with their clubs waving around above their heads. She wanted to find it funny, she really wanted to laugh at them but the clubs in their hands and the skins hanging around the fire made her think otherwise.

"SHHHHHHUUUA!" Suddenly everyone stopped shouting hello and lowered their clubs, everyone turned to the largest hut in the village. "WHY YOU SHOUTING HALLO!" Cried a large, muscle bound man.

"IT'S HELLO CHIEF!" Shouted one of the men.

"HELLO?" Repeated the Chief, the man nodded. "HELLOOOOOO! WHO SAYS THIS WORD?" There was a whoosh of skins as everyone in the village turned and pointed to Raine. The Chief turned to Raine and thundered over to her, he was very tall as he came to a stop in front of her. He was a truly terrifying sight, Raine wanted to hide behind someone, anyone.

"Hunter, get down from there." Cat could be heard calling to Hunter to get off of the cloud before he jumped too high. Talia seemed just as scared of this hulk of a man as she, so that was no help at all.

"WHAT IS THIS HELLO?" Thundered the Chief.

"Please allow me to," Talia took a small step forward to introduce them but the Chief was not having it, he held his large hand in front of her and shook his head.

"I NO SPEEK TO YOU SMALL WOMAN! I TALKING TO HER OF FIRE HEAD!" His attention returned to Raine once more, she jumped every time he opened his mouth to speak. His voice was by far the loudest thing she had ever heard in her life. Not even a fire work matched the booming voice before her, she felt it in her chest every time he opened his mouth. "WHAT THIS HALLO MEAN?" He shouted.

"Umm, well. It means. It's a greeting."

"GREETING WITH HELLO?"

"Yes, greeting with hello, to say hi, a greeting, friendly greeting, see?" The Chief pulled on his red beard and shook his head. He had the same thinking pattern of Hunter, taking a long time before his reply.

"ME NO SEE, WHY GREET WITH WORD, WHY NOT HEAD BUTT LIKE NORMAL PEOPLE?" He bellowed, Raine took a step forward and shook her hands hoping her was not about to head butt hers clean off her shoulders.

"No, no, not head butt, that would hurt."

"WHAT?"

"I said." Raine sighed and thought quickly, this seemed endless, surely there was a better way to get through to him what she was trying to say. That was it, Raine turned to the Chief, who stood waiting for her to reply, and took a deep breath. "I SAID NO HEAD BUTT," Everyone seemed stunned by the loud voice coming from her, even she was amazed at how loud she really was as she continued with glee. She had never been allowed to shot this loud, and strangely enough it did not hurt her throat, it felt natural to her. "THAT WOULD HURT. I WANT TO BE SEEING MAN IN CHARGE, THAT YOU?" The Chief looked at her for a moment with his arms crossed over his large chest. The village was silent apart from Hunter's cried of glee as he continually bounce of the ever thinning cloud.

"HAHAHA, YOU FIRE HEAD VERY GOOD TALKER, NO STORNG HEADS BUT LOUDS, I LEADER OF IGNIS. WHAT YOU WANTINGS?" Finally she was getting somewhere, it seemed the phrase, if you can't beat them join them really was true.

Raine took another deep breath and explained why they were there, she introduced Talia, Cat and Hunter. She explained about Auran and his mist, she told him how Terrae was lost and that she and Hunter was going to marry so she could go and seal him away forever.

"SO WE COME FOR BLESSINGS FROM YOUR REALM AND

SEAL FOR SEALING, YES?"

"NO." The Chief unfolded his arms and turned away from Raine without another word, she was not going to leave it as that, she ran in front of the hulking great mass and barred his way.

"WHY?"

"BECAUSE YOU SMALL PUNY WEAKLINGS, IGNIS FIGHT AURAN WHEN HE COME, WE NO FEAR, WE NO FALLINGS. BUT NOT BLESSINGS YOU HAVINGS AND NOT SEAL. DANCE MORE, IGNORE FIRE HEAD." Raine crossed her arms and felt herself become a little hotter than usual. She took another deep breath and refused to give up.

"NO NOT IGNORING FIRE HEAD." If that was how he was going to play then she would have to play too. Why did she have the idea that this realm was going to be harder to gain blessings from than the other two? "FIRE HEAD DEMANDS BLESSING FOR WEDDING AND SEAL FOR SEALINGS OF AURAN. I DEMAND IT NOW." The Chief turned back to Raine, his people muttered with excitement, maybe no one ever challenged his word like this, maybe this was more entertaining than running around the fire, waving clubs, chanting random words.

"WELL YOU FIGHT FOR IT, YOU WIN I GIVE BLESSINGS AND SEAL."

"But I can't fight you, your bigger than me." Said Raine a little deflated, her shouting voice had left her now. How could someone so small like her fight a man more than twice her size? And she had never fought with no one before in her life, she would rather talk about problems, or shout about them, but never fight them out like savages.

"I will fight him." Hunter jumped off the cloud as it disappeared and walked over to Raine and the Chief.

"WHAT, YOU? HAHAHA, YOU SO SMALL FOR MAN, YOU FIGHT?" Hunter ignored the laughing and picked up a club from the floor, the Chief stopped laughing and nodded. As he walked over to his hut to collect his own club Raine pulled Hunter to one side.

"What are you doing, he's bigger and stronger than you, you'll get hurt." But Hunter shook his head and tapped his nose with his finger giving her a knowing wink.

"You wait, you will see." With a mad smile, Hunter walked over to the waiting Chief leaving Raine to worry what he was thinking. She did not want to see him get hurt, after all she did care about him.

"WE FIGHT, FIRST TO FALL LOOSES. YOU WIN FOR FIRE HEAD AND GET BLESSING AND SEALING SEAL. YOU LOOSE, I GET FIRE HEAD FOR WIFE."

"WHAT?" Raine said startled, Hunter just grinned and nodded his agreement. Was he completely mad, then it hit her, yes he was mad, even with a small amount of sanity in that head of his, he was still mad. "Cat, do something, I don't want to be his wife." But all Cat could do was shrug, there was nothing any of them could do as Hunter took his coat off and put the club over his shoulder.

"READY!" He cried, the village erupted in sound, they surrounded the Chief and Hunter as they began to circle one another.

"Oh Hunter, I can't watch." Raine placed her hands over her eyes, but she could not help herself as she peeked through her fingers. The Chief raised his club above his head and ran towards Hunter, the ground shook, rocks jumped as he came closer and closer to Hunter. "MOVE HUNTER!" Cried Raine, but it was deafening over the sound of the villagers.

But Hunter did not move, he grinned insanely until the Chief was in front of him, he took a graceful sideways step as the Chief swung his club down. It hit the floor with a thud making Raine wonder what it could have done to Hunter's head, Hunter himself turned around and lifted his own club.

"TAKE THAT!" He cried hitting the Chief on the head. There was a stunned silence, everyone in the village let their mouths fall open as the Chief dropped his own club.

"OW!" He reached for his head and let out a large, long howl. "OOOOOUCH!" He began to cry large gravely tears as he sat down on the ground. Talia, Cat and Raine cheered and ran over to Hunter who grinned. "CHEAT, CHEAT. NO BLESSINGS. NO SEALINGS." The Chief got to his feet and knocked over several of his villagers as he ran into his hut. The villagers got to their feet once more and looked at one another.

"CRY, CRY,CRY!" They all began to shout, once again waving their club above their heads, no one was interested in the fight, or lack of fight and no one seemed to care that the Chief had gone back on his word.

"Well I must say Hunter that was a turn up for the books, I can't believe you beat him." Said Cat over the sound of CRY from the dancing villagers.

"That was most clever of you to move and hit his head. But I am afraid he will not give up his seal and not bless you. He seems quite, dishevelled." Raine nodded, he had been made a fool of in front of his entire village. Maybe she should go and talk to him, or shout, what was best?

"I'll go and talk to him, don't worry." Hunter gave Raine the club, which she instantly dropped through its size and weight, and walked over to the Chiefs hut. How on earth did Hunter hold this thing, he was clearly stronger than he looked.

"What do you think will happen?" Asked Talia, Raine shrugged, it was hard to tell with Hunter, he seemed to change with every passing second, she wondered if she would ever get used to it. "I only hope he does not injure his pride further. The people of Ignis are a very proud race you understand." Raine and Cat nodded their agreement. The dancing went on as they sat and waited, maybe it was because of the shouting villagers, or maybe the drums or maybe it was the erupting volcano nearby, but no one could hear Hunter's voice shouting at the Chief.

After the fight the villagers became very friendly, mostly towards Raine, they addressed her as Fire Head and piled them up with food and water. One set of women even gave them all a set of walking shoes for their journey to the Water realm. Raine ate and drank what they offered her, all the while her eyes looked to the hut. She was so worried, nothing could be heard from the hut. What was Hunter doing in there?

"THIS IS GOOD THEN?" Everyone looked up, Hunter and the Chief walked out of his hut like brothers in arms, laughing loudly, shouting at one another.

"YES!"

"THEN IT IS SETTLED, YOU AND FIRE HEAD RETURN ONE DAY AND WE DANCE, WAVE CLUBBINGS AND CELEBRATE!" Hunter nodded, shook the Chiefs hand and walked over to Raine.

"Here you go." He handed her a small volcano, the seal of Ignis, he had got it from the Chief. "And he gives us many big blessings on day of union and sealing's."

"Oh Hunter, good boy." Hunter smiled and clapped his hands, he seemed very pleased with himself, and so he should be. Raine was very impressed, he was not that mad, maybe a little mad, but not completely. Whatever he said to the Chief he said was going to keep a secret because no matter what Cat said or how nicely Talia requested, he never told them a thing. While Raine, she was just happy to keep guessing, she wanted to keep wondering how this man who could never hurt a fly, overpower and convince a man like the Chief of Ignis to part with his seal and grant his blessings.

After their trip to the village in the fire realm Raine began to feel tired, she wished they could stop and rest for a little while. But Cat told her that once they had the blessings and seal of the final realm they could return home and rest before the wedding. That made her feel a little better knowing she could at least rest before the wedding.

She did not feel any different knowing she and Hunter were to be married, it was a marriage to help the world, they were to complete a Union, confront Auran and either seal or somehow convince him to stand down.

If she was being honest with herself it was the thought of confronting Auran that scared her more, she had warmed to the idea of marrying Hunter after their talk in Wuffle's wood. She had never spoken to him in such an adult way before, he was a different man.

"I wonder what will happen after all this." She thought to herself as they walked along the fiery edge of a river of fire. "Will you want me to stay and be your wife, or will we go back to how we were? I'm not sure what I want, my mind can't get passed Auran." Raine looked at Hunter, he walked beside her, his hand tightly secured in her own while lightly humming to himself. "What if we don't make it, what if one of us," But she could not think like that, she had to stay positive. After all, if she had fallen every time she had a negative thought when she planned her escape from home, she would not be back with Hunter. "I just wish I knew."

"Raine," Talia placed her hand softly on Raine's shoulder making her jump slightly. "Are you well, shall we stop and eat, you look a little pail." Cat stopped and looked at Raine, he nodded his agreement and chose to sit away from the fiery lake.

"I have tea cake." Said Hunter reaching inside his bag, he pulled out four brightly coloured tea cakes and four plates with a large grin.

"It would seem I have bottles of coloured water, very bright I must say, Cat you are quite the culinary genius." Cat smiled and handed out sandwiches, it was a lovely little picnic and the bottle of coloured water made Raine feel much better.

"It is a new potion I created, it gives you energy through the natural properties found within the roots living within many plants in my field. I never knew it would be so handy darling, the colour has returned to your cheeks already." Cat was very pleased with himself as they all finished their bottles.

"Well, I must say, it is very genius, is there no potion you cannot make to aid us?" Cat thought for a moment, his wizard mind racing through the many possibilities.

"Well, I can't make life return to the dead, nor grant wishes, but thus far I have not failed. Let us be gone now, it is not far to the edge of Aqua I do wish to hurry, I hate water." Everyone laughed and got to their feet, it was nice to see that even though Cat seemed to appear and act human, he was still a feline at heart.

"I love the water, I remember when I first met Raine, she couldn't swim, so I taught her. She was very funny. I thought because her name was Raine that she could swim, but she couldn't, so I had to teach her." Talia looked to Raine with a small smile, Hunter continued to carry on explaining how Raine could not swim, and how he taught her for so long that the two girls decided to ignore him and talk about the realm of Aqua.

"Once we have finished our business here," said Cat as they reached the edge of Aqua. "We shall have to catch the tide to Vitam, but we will have to stay away from the current that takes us to the island, we do not want to be caught in that one. I don't think turtles will be a wise mode of transportation. Then we shall returned home and rest before the wedding tomorrow." Cat rummaged through his bag and handed everyone a bottle each, he had come fully prepared. "This bottle will give us a bubble of renewing air, if you swim within it you shall move the bubble. It will not last forever, but it has enough life to last for what we need to do."

"Well, let's go!" Hunter held his potion bottle high and jumped into the water, Talia looked to Raine and shrugged her shoulders before jumping in after him.

"Cat," he stood beside her and looked out to the vast body of water that was Aqua, he took her hand and nodded.

"I know, it will be fine Raine. You will be fine." He seemed to know what she was thinking, with a feline smile he jumped into the after leaving her to look over the calm depts.

It was the fog that had caught her eye, it seemed Auran had chosen his next conquest, but she would not let it happen, she refused to let him win. The rolling fog building up in the distance only made her resolve burn brighter.

"Well, trust magic I guess." She had never been a girl of magic, even knowing a wizard Cat did not help that, yet she would rather place her trust in Cat then in anything else. Raine jumped into the water expecting it to be cold, yet she was pleasantly surprised as to how warm it was.

She opened the bottle and watched happily as a bubble flew out and encased her in a comforting air bubble. It was strange, she knew she was in water, her brain told her she should not be breathing like this. "That's the wonder of magic." She smiled watching Hunter try and right himself, Cat swam by and pointed downwards indicating for everyone to follow him.

It was very peaceful swimming through the water like this, not having to worry about air, but through this peacefulness came one shuddering thought. "Where are all the fish?" Raine noticed that not one fish had swum by, there was no large fish, no mammals, nothing.

"It would seem Auran's fog has started to affect Aqua," said Cat.

"This is how our land started, the smaller creatures faded first while others fled to me." So Auran had started his attack on Aqua which meant he was getting strong and it was only a matter of time before he would move on.

"Then we need to hurry." Cat nodded and began to speed up, Hunter and Talia joined them and swam deeper into the abyss. Cat seemed to know where he was going, maybe it was that book because he confessed he had no desire to ever visit the realm of water.

It seemed they were headed for a coral reef, it was larger than any she had ever seen on documentaries, it was bright and beautiful. She swam up to a bright star shaped piece and reached out to touch it.

"Hay, what do you think you are up to? You do not belong here do you?" Raine suddenly jumped back as a small fish jumped out at her, pointing its fin at her. "I do not think that you should be here, for most of us we live in fear."

"Why are you talking in rhyme?" Asked Raine.

"It's common knowledge that in the sea, we all talk together in harmony." That was right, she did remember now that the people of the realm of water loved words, so they sung? It was very nice to hear, after all sound seemed to travel nicely for whales.

"Please tell me, is the King here, we need to talk to him, it's very urgent." The little fish looked at Raine, he seemed to be pondering, thinking.

"What would you want if I were to agree, for a royal invite is not easy to obtain you see." Raine sighed deeply and began to explain about Auran, his fog, their wedding and their plan to confront Auran. Would she ever stop telling the same story over again? "And you have gained the others ear, to show them you have no fear. For you I must openly admit, your plan is a little miss and hit." Surly he meant hit and miss, but he rhymed, it must be very hard to constantly think of words to rhyme in such a short time. "Yet I will tell you that in my heart, I can see in your eyes you speak from the heart. For you I shall grant the seal that is mine, and then bless you in all ways divine." So this was the King, this little fish. Talia and Cat swam over pulling Hunter along as they did, Talia bowed her head to the King. So she knew this King too, she was really a lady of knowledge.

"I beg of you to aid us dear King, you are the final seal and blessing we need in order to marry them and confront Auran." The King held his fin in front of him and shook his head.

"I have already spoken to Raine right here, for she has a heart open, so full, so dear. For the kingdom of Aqua can always see true, even though our kingdom is that of blue. For my seal and my blessing I ask only this, that you answer a riddle and then I shall assist." A riddle, they could answer a riddle for the seal, it was a lot easier than sending Hunter off to fight a Chief twice his size.

"Ask away." She smiled. The little fish nodded and revealed a devilish smile before opening his mouth with his riddle.

"What has holes, yet can still hold water fully?"

"What?" Raine turned to Talia, she was thinking sometime easy, but something that had holes yet still held water, that was hard.

"Does it leek?" Asked Talia, the King shook his head, so it wasn't a bucket with holes. "So it is whole, an object, but it has holes?" Talia seemed as stumped as Raine, she thought hard but nothing came to mind. Raine was never any good at riddles, she often paid no attention when her Aunt's played words games.

"Oh for heaven's sake." Cat swam back to the coral reef with Hunter's foot in his hand, he looked very irritated at the King. "If you are to ask a riddle, make it a challenge. The answer is a sponge."

"What?" Exclaimed Talia, Raine and the King. The little fish turned white for a moment, literally while in colour before he looked at Cat in disbelief.

"How can you solve my riddle without a clue, that riddle has never be solved by anyone but you. And without a thought you know the correct reply, I cannot say anything but let out a deep sigh. For I have been defeated in fair, now as agreed I will give you the seal so wait right there." Cat crossed his arms not looking in the least bit happy with himself. While Raine and Talia were left thinking how he swam up, heard the riddle and answered it while attending to Hunter.

"I'll be happier when you're married Raine, then you can take care of Hunter when he goes off, doing silly things like this." Raine smiled warmly, she knew Cat enjoyed fathering Hunter. It was a few moment later when the King returned with a lovely piece of coral, the seal of Aqua.

"Thank you very much, I promise to take good care of it and return it once we're successful." The little fish looked so unhappy, this made Raine want to stay and question his unhappy little face.

"I thought it would take you forever and a day, then I could have some company and might stay."

"Are you alone here?" The little fish nodded sadly and sat on his coral hole. Raine turned to Cat sadly and silently asked if she could bring him along with them.

"No, I will not have a fish in my house." He knew her so well as he shook his head and let go of Hunter's foot.

"But Cat, pleeeeease?"

"PLEEEEEASE!" Hunter joined in, the little fish looked up with a smile on his face, maybe he understood what Raine was asking.

"You would take me along so I was no longer alone?"

"If you stop rhyming Raine can take you, I'm sure I have a bottle in here somewhere we can place you in until we reach Terrae. But you're looking after him. I won't take responsibility for him, do I make myself clear?" Replied Cat as he started to swim back up wards, Hunter and Raine celebrated happily as the King swam out of his coral home and over to them.

"I am very happy and cannot thank you enough, I only hope our journey is smooth and not rough." Raine smiled and helped the little fish inside her bubble, Hunter let in a small amount of water in her bubble so he would not die and they all left to follow Cat.

The King's name was Walt, his mother had wanted to call him Walter but his father thought against it. He was the only one left on the reef, the others had left for waters further away from the fog. But he felt, as the King he should stay, it was his duty to protect his reef and his land.

He told Raine in song how the fog had come a few days ago and took many fish and creatures leaving very few in its wake. The few that were spared decided that it was unsafe to stay at the reef and left for safer waters with the mermaids leaving Walt alone.

"I cannot thank you enough for taking me along, I was beginning to think that place was not where I belong. To have such danger and to face it alone, it is not such a wise decisions for one accident prone." Raine smiled as they reached the banks of Terrae, the journey back through the waters of Aqua had been so easy without all the creatures around. They had found the current to take them back towards Vitam and with Cat's help they managed to avoid it and land safely back in the Earth realm.

"Finally, back of terra firma, I could not be happier. What say you darling?" Cat turned to Raine as she picked up the little water bubble with Walt inside.

"Oh yes, under the water is fun, but I was beginning to feel a little sick in there. Are you alright Hunter, Talia?" Both stepped out of their bubble and nodded their reply. Hunter yarned and stretched, he looked very tired, then again so did she, it had been a long journey and they must all be tired.

"I think we should return home, you and Hunter have a big day ahead of you, and you have to get married too." Cat smiled and pulled at Hunters leg. "Come with me Hunter, let's get you to bed."

"Then I shall take care of Lady Raine, come with me, I have a room for you to sleep in." Talia took Raine by the arm and began to lead her away from the field and towards the castle.

"See you in the morning Raine," called Hunter waving above his head, she returned his wave and smiled brightly at him until he was out of sight.

"Well, we are but half done." It was cold as they left Cat's field and entered the court yard of the castle. They had three of the four seal's needed to seal Auran away for good, but what about Jerrad's seal, what about Vitam's? Raine thought more about Auran then she did about her upcoming wedding, was that right? "Here, it may not be the grandest room at this time, but it was in its day." Raine stopped thinking about Auran and looked up, it was a dimly lit room and looked very old and neglected, but it was beautiful. "It has remained untouched since the days of Queen Terra. You see, Jerrad kept this room sealed away when he took the throne, he passed the key onto a maid and when she died passed it to my grandmother, and she passed it onto my mother and so on. I think, because you were his favourite, you should sleep in this room, and." Talia walked over to a large wooden cupboard and pulled open the doors. "When I was told of your wedding I told my lady in waiting to clean this for you, it is my gift to you."

"Oh Talia, I can't, it."

"No, please." Talia held out the beautiful white dress to Raine and shook her head. "I insist, apart from Cat and Hunter, you are the closet thing Jerrad had to family, he spoke fondly of you in the pages I have read. So, I think he would be happy to know you wear his sister's gown. This is the gown of grand occasions, imagine the balls she went to, the dances she waltzed. But we have had a long, tiresome day, and you must be fresh for your Union tomorrow. You do. Do you fully understand a Union?" Raine turned away from the dress and thought, it was a marriage like any other, they became man and wife and lived until death do us part? But Talia shook her head and took Raine to the sofa and sat her down. "In Ethernia, when you marry you are not only married in name, you are bound in heart and soul. Once the ceremony is complete you say a passage of words, once said by both of you, you must give the Kiss of Union." Kiss of Union, a real kiss. That was what Hunter was talking about, she found it strange how their kiss was not real to him. Now she knew why. "Yes, you will be forever united by your heart and souls, so no matter where you are in this world or another, you will always be untied, always together. Are you still happy to marry Hunter?" Forever, that was an awfully long time to be tied to someone. At least it made sense why people were forever bound to their partner until they died.

"Well, if our Union will help all of Ethernia and means I'm also bound forever to someone I care deeply for, then yes. Yes I'm more than happy to go through with it." Talia looked down and took her hand in hers.

"You are a brave woman, brave and loyal to a country and entire land that is not yours. I only wish one day I can be as strong as you."

"Talia, you are strong, in your own way. It took a lot to go against your bother and help me, you're a braver woman than I." Talia smiled and got to her feet, she bowed and told Raine that she would return in the morning with her hair maidens to prepare her for the wedding. She wanted Raine to have the perfect Union, it was the least Terrae could do for their saviour.

"Saviour hmm? I wouldn't go that far." Said Raine as Talia closed the door behind her. She began to look around the room, she could picture how grand and beautiful this room could have been before the fog.

The bed was still soft and fresh and this room was clearly kept clean and free of the withering world outside, but it was but a shadow of its former glory. "I wonder what Queen Terra was like?" thought Raine walking around the room, she let her hand fall on the back of a chair, she let it run along the dressing table and let it light fall as she walked back over to the bed. She was very tired and looked forward to falling asleep on that warm looking bed.

As she walked over to the bed she stopped, at the foot of the bed was a baby cradle, it was still new, white bedding lay on in while a pattern of leaves ran over the cradle. "How sad," said Raine running her hand over the cradle, not only had Auran killed his sister and her King, but it was clear now that Terra was with child. "Poor Jerrad, I wonder if he knew? Maybe he did, that was why he took a shining to me, he would have been an uncle." The thought of a life not coming into this world made her feel very sad indeed. Raine lay down on the bed and tried to push the thoughts of tomorrow out of her mind.

"Sleep is a vital part of life," Walt's voice suddenly drifted from beside her, she turned over and looked on the bedside table. A fish bowl was slowly forming with the little Fish King inside, he smiled and settled down in a make shift coral reef. "Without it our waken world would be full of strife." He swam to the edge of the bowl and smiled, he patted the bowl with his fin before retuning back to his coral. "Your friend Cat is very clever and smart, he is very well practiced within his art. But manners towards the watery kind is less than homely, I no doubt he is not fond of the foamy."

"You just made that up." Walt laughed and closed his eyes, now Raine knew this was a different world to her own, a fish to talk and have eye lids to sleep? This was truly a different world to her own, a world where everything had no rules and things rarely made sense. "But I would have it any other way." She smiled closing her eyes.

Chapter Seven

Raine and Hunter's Union

"Lady Raine keep still, please stop moving."

"Raine, are you nervous?" Talia sat on a chair behind Raine as her hair maidens dressed and made Raine look beautiful for her wedding. She was not nervous for the wedding, maybe she really did not fully understand what it meant to have a Union and that was why she did not worry.

"It's Auran, I hope." She closed her eyes as the last hair maiden put the finishing touches to her hair. She then got to her feet and walked over to the mirror, she could not help but smile and wish secretly that Aunt Maud, Iris, Pearl and Louie was here to see her. It would have been nice for them to see her on her wedding day. She knew they would be crying but not for sadness, for joy and happiness.

"Why, you look like a Queen Raine. There is just something about you that tells me so." Talia was dressed in a fine green dress ready to be her bridesmaid. Raine had on the white dress from Talia, that was her something borrowed for even in Ethernia they have the same tradition. Cat had sent over a tiara made from the coral of Walt's reef, that was a lovely blue colour, her something old was her necklace from Hunter and her something new was a flower she had asked for.

"I am very happy with your hair my Lady." Said the hair maiden, she was too. It was flowing with green vines running though it making it look so full of volume she thought her hair had doubled in size.

"Well Raine, shall we? If you are ready that is?" Raine took one last look at herself in the mirror and closed her eyes in thought. This was it, after this, they would go to Vitam, and confront Auran, she hoped it would end well.

"Alright. Let's go." This was it, her heart and soul would be united forever with Hunter's, she could unite with anyone in this world or hers and for many other reasons other than love. But as she travelled Ethernia she realised, there were greater reasons to unite than for love.

"Cat has really made this field beautiful." Raine could feel herself start to feel light on her feet, she was. Excited. "And look Lady Raine," Talia pointed to the windmill, it was beautiful. Raine could not help but gasp, she felt a tear fall down her cheek as they walked towards the windmill.

There were so many people and creatures gathered, they were not only from Terrae, but from the other realms too.

"My lady Raine." King Foog bowed as she walked passed him and a few of his people, they were all dressed in fine yellow robes. After she walked passed them she had to cover her ears as the people of Ignis shouted their greetings.

"FIRE HEAD." The Chief was there too with his people, the fight with Hunter had not dampened his spirits as he joined in with his people. Even the people and creatures from Aqua had joined them, small and large bubble of water sat around the field, clearly Cat had been busy.

And waiting for her was Cat, dressed head to paw in a fine suit and top hat, he stood at the end of the isle he had left for her, with a smiled he bowed and held his paw out to her.

"It would be my honour to take you down the aisle." Raine smiled in return and took his waiting paw, he must have taken another potion because he was now slightly taller than her. "After we visited the realms they all made their way here, it was impossible to stop them. And he has been very excited all night and morning. I don't think he got much sleep." Cat motioned towards the front where a beautiful archway full of vines, flowers and all sorts of greenery stood, and there waiting for her with Dallan was Hunter. "Are you ready Raine?" Cat placed his paw on her hand and waited for her, she did not need to think, she smiled and nodded. With a proud smile Cat turned to a group of Wuffle's and waved his free paw, they began to place music and it begun.

"You look so grown up Hunter." Thought Raine as she walked towards him. His green suit was perfect, there was not one thing about him that looked mismatched today. His hair was combed nicely, he wore a top hat and a tie. "Are you sure you want to do this too Hunter, you look so happy I can't tell what's going on in your mind." Then they came to a stop in front of him, Hunter smiled from ear to ear and held his hand out. Waiting.

"Good luck." Whispered Cat placing her hand in Hunter's, that was it, she was given away and now they would marry. Hunter mouthed 'hello' to her and smiled before turning to face Dallan.

"Today we are all gathered to witness and bless this Union of Hunter of Terrae and Raine of the far off land." Dallan looked over the field of all creatures and people as the music stopped and everyone sat down. "For this, today, this is not simply a Union of wedlock, not only is this Union for the love of these two hearts. It is a Union to save our world of Ethernia and that Union is the most sacred of them all." Hunter squeezed her hand tightly as Dallan began to ceremony. He began to speak of each blessing from the other realms, with each mention of the blessing Raine could feel her chest warm. With every word spoken she could hear a second heart beating with her own, was that Hunter's heart beating in time with hers? "Hunter, Raine join your hands and we shall start the Union." Raine took Hunter's left hand in her own left hand and looked to Dallan, Talia had taken her through all of the ceremony and this point, the Union.

"It's more than just a Kiss, the words, your heart and soul must be in union with Hunter's or it will fail and you never have the chance to do it again. Listen to him, listen to his heart and you will unite." She had said, but it was easier said than done as Raine felt her chest become so warm she could not help but place her hand on in.

"You feel it too?" Asked Hunter in a whisper, Raine nodded her reply and let him take her free hand, he placed it on his own burning chest and smiled. "For you Raine."

"Please, stop talking, replace your hands, but keep the left united." Whispered Dallan with a kindly smile.

"Sorry." Both Raine and Hunter smiled and laughed secretly. She could see the happiness in the old man's eyes, he looked. Touched.

"Now, feel the others heartbeat, feel the fire grow, let it flow like water and breath like the wind until it is solid as a rock. Let her life be yours Hunter, Raine let his soul flow from him and live within you." Raine looked down at their links hands, with every word she listened and let her heart beat, she invited Hunter's heart with an open soul. Their hands began to glow, one, two, three and four balls of light began to circle their linked hands as Dallan continued with is words telling them welcome the other, to feel their hearts as one. "Now, both of you must speak the words of Union and seal your Union with Unions Kiss." What a lot of Union in that sentence, thought Raine as she looked to Hunter, together they must speak the words of Union.

"May the four elements forever bless our hands, our heart and souls from this day fourth unite as one. From this moment I pledge my life to thee, with a Kiss of Union I am complete with thee." They were perfect, they took breaths at the same moment, they spoke in unison as they completed the ceremony and now that left one last thing.

"The kiss." She thought, Hunter began to blush as he held her hand tighter, she gently pulled him by the hand telling him she was shy too. Hunter smiled and took a step forward, his free hand reaching for her cheek as she felt her heart pound against her chest.

Suddenly, as their lips were inches apart, the ground began to shake, people began to scream as the earth began to crack and a dense fog began shooting from the ground. Hunter pulled Raine closer to his and wrapped his arms around her as one crack emitted a fog that took the form of a person, a man. It looked over the people and creatures and they ran and finally stopped on them.

"So, I have finally broken through the cat's defences, the last part of Terrae."

"Auran?" Raine looked at Hunter, he looked angry as his eyes burned towards the figure hovering over them.

"And you must be the outsider who wanted to come and see me, yes I know all about your little union, the little, fat King told me all about it when I questioned him about my offering." Auran was not solid, he was like a ghost, his green eyes burned brightly as they fixed themselves on Raine. "Do you really think by having a Union with this man you will be able to talk to me?" Raine pulled herself from Hunter's grip and walked towards Auran's ghost like figure.

"I hoped so," she said, still feeling Hunter's heart beating, but now it was angry, she could feel his anger deep within her chest. The Union was not complete. "I wanted to talk with you myself, I wanted to know why you wanted to harm Terrae so much. Surely you love this land like your brother and sister? I know you were over looked for the throne, but surely now, after all these years you can let go. Maybe you can come to Terrae, help restore the damage you have done and rule your old region? It doesn't have to be this way." Auran looked down, he closed his eyes and hummed slightly before returning his gaze to her. She felt so small as his ghost towered over her.

"You know, my sister Terra said the same thing before she died, she said to me, 'Brother, you must stop this madness, Terrae has always been ruled by women it is the way. But together we rule, with me as the Queen and you as my Brother, please, Auran, it doesn't have to be this way.' That was her last words to me before she died." They were very kind and worthy words from a sister, not a Queen, even Raine could see from that Terra loved her Brother. But Auran smiled, his eyes did not tell her he was considering her words, he began to laugh softly, then he burst into a fit of laughter. "I told her then and I shall tell you now, I will not settle for a region of a land that should be mine. Not only that I will not stand and let Vitam remain empty when I could sit upon its throne. Little underling of the other world, I shall take this one and then your own."

"Raine!" Auran lifted his hand and swiped down towards Raine, Hunter ran to her side and pushed her to the floor before being flung into their archway. She looked to Hunter, he was alright, he tried to get up but fell under the archway.

"No new husband to protect you now." Auran lifted his hand again, his eyes blazing widely. "Argh!" Balls of green light flew out of nowhere and hit Auran in the chest. Then a yellow and red hit him followed by a blue.

"Raine, get up, now."

"Louie, what are you doing here?" Raine could not believe her eyes as Louie sat beside her and tried to pull her to her feet.

"Come on, there's not time to waste we have to go." He began to pull her away, she realised it was away from the windmill, away from Hunter. Away from Terrae.

"Louie, no." She pulled her hand away and stood her ground, she was not a child anymore and she was married now, she had to go to Hunter.

"Louie, why are you still here with her, Raine, go back to the window with Louie and," Aunt Pearl joined them as Aunt Iris and Maud threw magic balls at the ghost of Auran. He wailed in pain as they continued to attack him leaving the others to run to safety.

"No, I have to go back to Hunter." She dodged Louie's hand and ran to the fallen archway, she fell to Hunter's side and pulled him onto her lap. There was a loud moan and the ground rumbled again, she did not want to see what was going to happen. She closed her eyes and covered Hunter with herself, if they were to die together then so be it, even if they had not fully finished the Union.

The ground stopped shaking, was it all over now, Hunter opened his eyes to find himself in Cat's field in some sort of bed. He was looking up at the sky, but it was no longer a happy blue, it was grey and sad. Then something reminded him.

"Where is Raine? Cat, Cat where's Raine, I can't hear her." Cat was tending to the fire Chief's head, he gave him a bottle and wandered over to him. "Where's Raine, why can't I hear her Cat?"

"Calm down Hunter, please, drink this, the Union was not complete, your married, but." Hunter took the bottle and drunk it, he then got to his feet and looked around the field. He did not care about the ruined grass, the dead flowers or the people all around. He wanted to find Raine, he wanted to know where she was and why he could not hear her.

"I don't care," There she was, she walked out of the remains of Cat's wind mill followed by four elemental pixies, it had been so long since he had seen one, or had he just remembered them from Jerrad's tales? "I'm not going home, I'm not leaving Ethernia with you." She was so angry, he could feel that much now. She was such a fire head now, she shouted like a lady from Ignis.

"Raine." Her angry little face turned to him and smiled, he ran over to her and hugged her tightly, he was so happy she was alive. He was scared she might have been hurt badly. "I'm glad you're safe, you're crazier than me for trying to talk to Auran, he's very mean." Suddenly the Fire pixie grabbed Raine's hand and held it up, he was a very angry pixie.

"What is this, what have you done?" He demanded, Raine looked to Hunter.

"We. We got married."

"You had a Union?" Cried the Air Pixie.

"Well we did," said Hunter looking at their glowing hands, the balls still circled them even though they were not joined together anymore. "But we haven't done the Union Kiss, Auran came and,"

"You. Got. Married?"

"Auntie Pearl, don't be sad." These were her aunties and Louie, that did not make sense even to him, they were elemental pixies. "I wanted to see Auran to stop this from happening, but the King said no so Hunter said he would marry me. So we went to the other realms, got blessings and seals and came back. We got married but didn't get to Union Kiss so we're only half married. But," She took a deep breath and stood by him and Cat with a look he had never seen before. "I don't care what you say or want to say,"

"What was you thinking, you'll have to Unite with him, you'll be in a state of Union forever. Your heart and souls will be,"

"United forever I know, I understand Louie but you don't understand, I'm going now with Cat, Hunter and Talia to Vitam and we're going to seal Auran away forever, we have to do it now." Cat nodded while Raine stood firm, she was a real grown up lady now. How did he miss her grow up so fast?

"Raine you can't stay here, you have to,"

"No. Hunter is my husband now and we will complete our Union once we have gone to Vitam."

"But what if you die?" Said the pixie called Louie, But Hunter would not let Raine answer, he put his arm around his wife and pulled her close to him.

"I won't let her die." He could hear her now, her heart fluttered like a butterfly, maybe he would go and catch one for her when they had all finished. Raine liked butterflies.

Chapter Eight

The Lost Firefly

After a heated war of words with her Aunties and Louie, Raine decided that she would finish what she started. As Hunter said he would not let her die she felt her heart flutter within her chest, she smiled at him and took his waiting hand. He was so grown up, she could now feel his heart even though they were not fully united.

Together with Cat and Talia, they went to the bank of Terrae's last river and looked over to the foggy island that was Vitam. This was it, Cat had the royal Seal's in his bag, he would be helping Raine complete the ritual that would seal Auran, this time she hoped it would be forever.

"I have read the book on Union and it says that your Union should hold him firm, even though it was not complete you are still half way there darling. Are you sure you want to do this?" Asked Cat as Hunter pulled the boat out of the reeds. Raine nodded her head and looked at Vitam, it was such a sad thing, Auran was Jerrad's Brother, she had been very fond of Jerrad when he was alive.

"It has to be done." She replied as Talia stepped into the boat, she did not need to come, she had done all she could in helping with the other Realms, but she wanted to come in hopes that the lost Earth Seal would be replaced by her presents.

"Come on, let's go." Hunter helped Cat and Raine into the boat before he picked up the ores. It was very cold as they got closer to Vitam, the wind whistled in her ears with an eerie whisper. "It's very different to last time." Raine nodded, the playground was gone, ghosts floated around without any purpose in their glides. She could hear distant voices saying words she could not understand.

"Monstrous." Whispered Cat as his eyes searched the land before them, Raine shivered as they walked out of the dock yard area and began to walk through the fog. "We need to find the centre, no doubt Auran will be waiting there for us. I have been reading and the books say that the centre of Ethernia is Vitam, and that its power comes from the centre of the island, was there a castle when you came here?" There was, she and Hunter had danced until they fell, Raine has kissed Hunter's cheek and they fell asleep. That was the last time they had seen one another, she could never forget that day.

"Castle, that's the centre. Hunter, we fell asleep in that castle. Well the remains." Raine stopped walking and realised something. "Cat, was Auran sealed in the castle?"

"Yes he was, why didn't you tell us you were in the castle, here in Vitam?" Raine closed her eyes, it really was her fault. They had gone into the castle, maybe by going into the ruined castle it had somehow woken Auran and caused a chain reaction that started all this.

As she let her thoughts carry on and away with her she felt a pair of arms go around her, they pulled her against their chest and held her tightly.

"It wasn't your fault darling." Came Cat's voice.

"You really can't blame yourself, you have no magical power to open his seal and neither does Hunter, so it is quite impossible for it to be your fault." Added Talia.

"But there you are quite wrong." Raine buried herself further in the arms and wished Auran would go away.

"Hunter." She whispered, but Hunter was the strong one now, he cupped her face in his hands and smiled before he rubbed her tears away. She could hear his heart beating, it beat strong and fast as he took her hands and pulled her towards the remains of the castle of Vitam.

"You see," Auran's voice echoed all around them like the wind, it sent shivers down her spine as they continued getting closer to the castle. "It was you who came to this island, and I knew you would come back again to try and seal me."

"How was it Raine's fault you were free?" Asked Cat into the air, everyone was being so strong, she was scared, she wanted to turn around and go home. Why was everyone so brave and she suddenly felt hers leaving her?

"Well, let me tell you a story, I bet your dying to hear it." He laughed and sent a cold wind, slapping her back, but Hunter pulled her tighter and they pushed on. "Three children were in line for the Throne of Terrae, but only the girl was given the throne, leaving the oldest to wait for the day she would possibly die. But she never did, even a talk of their mothers misdeeds did not give him the throne."

"The realm of Earth has always been ruled by females, earth is a kind and gentle element and the beginnings for us all, that is why it is called mother earth, Gaia. That is why you was never to be King, we start life wither within a female or in the ground, and when we die we return to the earth." Cried Cat full of rage, she had never seen him so angry. Raine saw the castle, they had to walk through the court yard and then.

"But I was the oldest!" Cried Auran. Would he be waiting for them, would he kill them, what if they failed? Raine felt everything they had worked for finally come true, it was happening, it was really happening. "I had to have a throne of my own. So, this brother, he was angry at his sisters pitiful present of a region and decided to look into another rule. And so he found Vitam, so he destroyed that land and took it for himself and started a war."

"But why, why didn't you stay with your own region and wait, maybe the Queen would have given up the throne, you could have lived longer." Raine called into the air, they were so close to the castle now, another few steps and they would be inside.

"BUT THAT WAS IMPOSSIBLE!" Auran's rage shook the walls of the castle as they walked inside the dead hall. If it had been under different circumstances, Raine would have been happy to come back. She remembered dancing with Hunter here with some fondness. It always made her smile when she remembered him. "You see, my dear sister was with child." Raine knew that, she had seen the cradle and felt sorrow, and now anger as Auran laughed again. "I knew once that child was born I would have no chance of getting Terrae's throne. But now," They were there, this was the throne room to Vitam, this was where she had fallen asleep with Hunter, and this would be where they would seal Auran away forever.

"I hope,"

"Raine!" She turned to Cat as Auran's solid form sat on the broken marble throne before them. "Do not doubt darling, you must keep your heart strong, stay strong." Raine nodded and looked to Auran, his very appearance made her scared, she felt a chill run though her.

"But now the Child of Life is here and wants to seal me away, and you even bought your little friends to. But you see, I too have little friends." Auran held his hand up and ghosts surrounded them, Cat sighed sadly, muttering he knew some of the ghosts.

"Well, its time." Hunter let go of Raine's hand and stood before Auran, he looked towards Auran's throne and pulled out a long stick.

"Hunter what are you," but Cat pulled her back and shook his head. "But Auran will,"

"No time, here are the seals, try your best to seal him away, Dallan is looking for a way to bypass the last seal but you have to start now. Talia and I shall hold off these ghosts with my potions but you MUST do it Raine." Cat thrust the bag with the seals into her hand and turned to the surrounding ghosts, he left Raine alone.

Hunter was fighting with Auran, he was brave. Talia and Cat threw potion bottles at the ghosts trying to keep them away from her. They were being brave. But she was not brave or smart, Raine looked to the seals in the bag and felt her heart jump, she turned to Hunter.

"I hear you." She nodded towards him and ran over the centre of the throne room, she knelt beside the hole where Auran had once been sealed. There were four slots for the royal seals, but what was the hole for, maybe it closed up once she completed the ritual. "May the air within grant the swift," she placed the seal of A'ris in its place. "With the waters to wash the dark away," that was the Aqua seal, now for the Ignis seal. "For the fires to burn the ghost away." There, now what, she needed the last seal from Terrae.

"Raine look out!" Cat cried, she looked up from the seals and closed her eyes as a ghost flew towards her.

"Stay away from my niece!" That was Aunt Pearl's voice, she opened her eyes and looked up. The three Aunt's and Louie surrounded her, each holding a wand, now each with a set of wings a different colour. "Are you alright my love?" Asked Pearl kneeling beside her.

"Yes, but the last seal, did Dallan tell you anything?" Aunt Iris, Maud and Louie began throwing magic balls at the ghosts while Aunt Pearl nodded and reached for the tree around her neck.

"This, Jerrad gave it to you correct?" Raine nodded looked to the tree, it was her key for getting in and out of Ethernia.

Then something hit her, something she had not registered before back in Cat's field, she looked to her Aunt's and Louie, then back to Aunt Pearl.

"What are you doing here, how did you know I was in Ethernia?" Aunt Pearl looked to Iris, then Maud and finally Louie.

"For heaven's sake just tell her everything." Said Louie over his shoulder. "And make it fast, Hunter's not fairing too well, but Cat is going to help him so don't worry." Aunt Pearl turned back to Raine and pulled her back down as she tried to go and help Hunter.

"Raine dear, if you use the Earth seal it will break along with the rest, and although a new one will be created, the door only opens for Jerrad's seal. This one." Raine looked down at the seal, she would never be able to go home? "But, maybe this will help you decide. I'm sure you realised by now we are not of your world?" Raine nodded and turned back to Hunter and Cat, they were not doing so well, Cat's potions were helping Hunter but Auran was too strong. "Each of us are Pixies from each realm, Queen Terra, she was. She was your mother,"

"What!"

"Please, Raine. Once the war started she called and told us to take you far away, through the windows and through a door she made. Once we went through there was only one more journey left in it. Clearly you used it somehow, Jerrad gave you his seal, he knew who you were and from your diary I can see he loved you dearly and knew not to tell you."

"Pearl, you always take so long." Louie knelt beside her and took her hand, his eyes blazed with a fire she had only seen in the Fire realm. "You are a child of Life, your parents were two of each, when you seal him away it will be forever because of your birth. You can never go back home if you do and you would have the King of Terrae to contend with as you are the rightful Queen of both Terrae and Vitam. But whatever you decided, I, we are all behind you." He smiled and kissed her forehead. "You have been my daughter for all these years and I love you dearly, do what's in your heart."

"But she can never go home." Said Iris, but Raine held the tree in her hand, she looked up and smiled. She finally understood, she finally had the answers she had been looking for, for so long. It had been right there, right under her nose all the time. She simply did not know it.

"I am home." She looked up and hoped Hunter could hear her, he was mad, but he was brave, he was her husband and they were bond in Union. "May Mother earth seal you back whence you came, in Life's name." She placed the tree in its hole and held her breath, but nothing happened. She looked to Aunt Pearl, she shook her head but had to leave her as Iris called for her help. "Cat, what do I do, it didn't work." Cat fell to her side, he was hurt, he was bleeding. She felt her mind panic, she did not want him to die, blood scared her, it always meant death.

"Life, Life has not blessed." He closed his eyes and drew his breath deeply, Raine looked around her, everyone was fighting hard, she had failed, nothing happened when as she completed the ritual. But then she felt Hunter's heart, it stopped for a moment before jumping back.

"Hunter." Raine got to her feet as Cat pushed her, she ran passed her Aunt's and ignored their cries, she ran through the ghosts and passed Auran. "Hunter, Hunter open your eyes."

"Ouchy, I have a booboo." Raine smiled slightly and held him up, he had fought so hard and she could not be happier or more proud of him. "You. You shouldn't be here Raine, you could get hurt." He said taking her hand in his, she could feel his heart still inside her.

"I know, but your my husband," Hunter gripped her hand tightly with a smile.

"And you are my wife, my Princess of Terrae, yes I knew." He said with a knowing smile. "Jerrad told me after you left, he said you would come back one day, because you were Terra's daughter." She could hear Auran say something, whatever he said meant nothing to her as Hunter closed his eyes and nodded his head towards her.

"Hunter, I." What could she say, after all they had been through, after the adventures, the games, growing up together, what could she say right now, she loved him. She loved him? She did, how could she be so blind to that, why else would she come back, why else would she go to every realm to save Ethernia? Why would she have married him if deep down she did not love him? "Hunter," Raine smiled and reached for his cheek, she could feel his heart inside her as their lips touched. "I love you Hunter." She told him with her heart, she knew he could hear her, she could hear him say the same, he loved her too. That kiss felt strong, she felt herself fall until something held her tight.

As they looked at one another they smiled, they had completed the Union, she felt Hunter within her, their souls were one, she looked at their linked hands, she had forgotten they were together. "Hunter, Life, I'm the Life Princess, the seal." She held their hands in front of them and looked to Auran, that man was her Uncle, he had killed her Mother, tormented the land and everyone in it, he was no part of her family. Maybe once he was a true man before the power had turned him mad.

"What are you doing, how did you?" Auran held a sword up high, Hunter pulled Raine close to him as Auran pushed his sword down. That was all they could do, if the seal failed then she would happily die with Hunter there, in his arms, together. Raine closed her eyes and placed her head on Hunter's chest, she listened to his heart until.

Chapter Nine

So Many Moons and Suns Have passed.
(That's two years to me and you)

Cat woke to the sound of birds singing outside of his window, he rubbed his eyes with his paws and got up to his window.

"Shut up! I'm trying to sleep!" He yelled, the birds laughed and flew away as he started to throw empty bottles out of the window. "Might as well get up now, what a pancake." Cat dressed himself and made his way to his kitchen, it was rather lonely this morning in his field, he did not want to admit it but he rather enjoyed having all the refugees in his field. "It has been two years already, my, my, my how times flies." Cat reached up and pushed the pendulum of his clock as it had stopped again. He cursed it for being so lazy and decided to take tea outside, it was indeed a bright and beautiful day. The sun was in the sky playing with a nearby cloud while the birds flew around the field kissing the flowers as they dived one by one.

Cat was very happy Terrae was beautiful again, he had missed having his privacy but he missed the hum of creatures and people from before. "Talia is a very good Queen," he thought drinking his tea. The garden needed weeding, they had set up home in his roses again, naughty things they were, he would have to put more Weed Killer on the ground in future. "I wonder what the good Queen is doing today, maybe I shall visit her." Cat smiled and turned to the castle, it too was beautiful once more, covered in vines and flowers.

Yet, as his eyes fell on Hunter's tree house he felt a sadness in his heart, it was quite unused, it stood empty and quiet in the morning sun. "I miss you old boy." He said sitting down at his table, he closed the book on the table and did not feel like potion making, he missed how Hunter would wake him up with jelly, or how he screamed in the night that Pompom's were coming to get him. He even missed how Hunter drunk all of his fruit milk and left him none. His cups were in perfect order, Cat found himself dropping the odd cup lately, letting it break just for happier memories.

"Cat, Cat!" What was it now, could a cat not mope around in peace?

"Queen Talia, what do I owe the pleasure?" Talia jumped down off her horse and patted its nose before running over to Cat, she picked him up and twirled around in a circle. "This is most un-lady like, please remember you are a Queen Talia." But she did not seem to hear, she sat him down and returned to her horse with so much excitement he could not help but ask. "What is the matter?"

"Oh you don't know, I sent the birds to. Oh, you shooed them away didn't you?" Talia was becoming looser in her words, she was meant to be a Queen, a well spoke, well-mannered, lady like Queen.

"I hate the birds singing outside my windmill. But what was they to tell me?" He asked sitting back on his chair full of grumpiness. Why did everyone seem so happy today when he felt in a foul mood?

"Oh it's started, it's started!" IT? It had started? Why had she not said this sooner rather than jumping on and off horses, or spinning him around like a toy. Or worse. A house cat.

"Then we must go." Cat reached inside and began picking things up, he just threw them into a bag and rushed outside not waiting for Talia to join him. But her horse was fast, she kept up with him as they ran through his field. They ran passed the Wuffle's as they wandered around outside their woods, they ran passed the castle all the way to the last river of Terrae.

"You sure took your time, I have been waiting." Louie stood in the boat with ores looking at the sun, it shrugged back as Cat helped Talia into the boat. Clearly it was no impressed either.

"As fast as you can." Louie nodded and began to row, faster Cat thought faster or it would all be over.

"Need a hand?" Cat looked over the side, Walt poked his head up from the water and smiled, he waved his fin and a school of fish circled the boat. They propelled them forward towards the shining island of Vitam.

"I only hope we are not too late." Said Cat hopefully.

"Have faith, have faith." Said Louie with a smile.

Hunter stepped outside and onto a balcony, he wiped his brow and looked at the hanky.

"Yuck, salty." He said before looking out over the palace grounds. He liked living here, he felt a little lonely sometimes, there was always someone that was never there. He looked at his left hand and smiled, his Union, that would be the only time he would want a Union, he knew that. It had seemed like such a long time ago since it had happened. He felt sad at times when he thought about it, but happy at other times. "Oh, Cat's coming to see me, I wonder whatever for, he's running very fast, is he late?" Hunter turned and left the balcony, he would go and meet them and ask Cat what he was late for? "Maybe he had fruit milk, I could do with some fruit milk, and a tea cake. I like tea cake." Said Hunter as he walked to the top of the grand stairs.

"Hunter, there you are, we are not late?" Why was Cat asking him, how did he know what they were late for if no one told him. People really should remember what they were here for and not ask him, he had a terrible memory. Then he remembered.

"Oh yes that. Nope. Well yes. But nope. But then again it depends what you mean by late for, but nope."

"Hunter,"

"Hmm?" Cat took him by the collar and pulled him to one side.

"Have we missed it?" Hunter smiled and shook his head, it was over, but they had not missed anything at all. Cat sighed and asked him to lead the way, Hunter was surprised they wanted to go now, it was all messy, and hot, and very scary, but he was feeling better now Cat was here.

"You bought Louie and Talia." He said walking back down the corridor, Louie nodded, he had asked Louie to get Cat and Talia, that was right, he was so forgetful lately. "Here we are, not too loud now ok. Shhhh." Hunter opened the door to his room and let them walk in, he followed them and skipped over to the bed.

He had been so happy, he had thought Raine was dead after Auran's sword had touched her, but she had smiled and been ok after a few days in bed.

"Oh, Raine, they are beautiful." Hunter knew that, their Mother was beautiful so it was silly for their new born babies not to be. Talia walked over to Raine and placed a kiss on her head before giving one to each of the babies.

"Thank you." Raine looked super tired, he fainted as she began to push out the little baby, he then fainted when Pearl told them another baby was going to come out any moment after the first. He wanted to wait to see if another baby did come out, then he would faint.

"This is Terra, and Jerrad. I named the little boy see, I did want to call him Cat after Cat, but then I thoughts he a little baby boy not a Cat and it would be silly having a boy called Cat." Raine smiled as Hunter sat beside him and took the babies from her, he held them and walked over to Cat, he was very quiet now, he was never quite. Why was Cat so quiet if he always had something to say, unless he was reading. "Cat, are you ok?"

"Yes, I am." Was Cat crying, why did he cry if he was so happy, he was a daddy, he could teach them how to hunt for Pompom's in Wuffle's Wood and Cat could teach them how to make potions and magic and. "I am very proud of you Hunter. And you too Darling." Hunter smiled as baby Terra began to gurgle, she was so very talk-a-tive for a little baby, she was just like him. "And now, I have a few potions to help you Raine, but after that you will need your rest, will you be ok to help Raine Hunter, will you need any of us to stay?" Hunter looked around, then to his wife, she was so very beautiful and he loved her with all his heart and soul. But she knew that already, he did not need to tell her that in words.

"I love you too Hunter." Her heart said, Hunter sat back down on the bed after Cat had helped Raine with potions, he placed their little babies on the bed with them and cuddled up to his little family.

"Hunter," Cat stopped at the door, he said nothing, but Hunter knew what he was saying and for once, Hunter said nothing in return.

"I'm very sleepy." Whispered Raine as Jerrad snuggled up to his mother, he was such a mummy's baby already, snuggling up to her so much.

"So would I after pushing two little people out of my belly." Raine laughed gently and rested her head on his shoulder. "Don't worry, you sleep ok, Cat has left thingies Terra and Jerrad need. We'll be fine my Queen." Raine smiled and slowly let her breathing slow, she looked so very pretty when she was sleeping. Hunter looked down at his little family and felt happiness, he was a King now, a King of the entire country with five realms to rule and care for. Yet, as he looked back down at Raine, Terra and Jerrad he smiled. "I have the most important job right here." He said. "Protecting you three." Hunter closed his eyes and listened to Raine's heart beating softly, he liked to make sure she was still here with him. He listened closely, he waited and then.

"There they are." Whispered Raine as two little hearts joined their own melody, the newest additions to the Firefly family.

Chapter Ten

Ethernia's history part 368
as written by Cat of Terrae

Throughout my time on Ethernia I have seen many things, I have seen many great Rulers of the five realms, I have seen lazy ones, active ones and I have seen benevolent ones. But I can honestly say that I have never seen such a ruler as Raine Firefly. It was such a long hard road for her, but she took to the throne with such ease I cannot describe it.

I can remember the day she sealed Auran away as though it were yesterday, she sat with Hunter, Ghost wailed around her and the war had begun. I hoped in my heart it would end there and not spread to the other lands. Yet, all was not lost, Raine and Hunter had joined hands, their left hands, their Union hand and they kissed. My only guess is that kiss was pure love between them because it completed the Union between them. You see, I have read into my past work from my youth days and I once wrote that to seal such a negative soul as Auran, nothing short of the love shared at the moment of Union can complete it. For Raine to be of the Life blood line and the rightful Heir to Vitam, her wish to seal Auran completed the ritual and he was sealed deep within the core of Ethernia, never to rise again. You see, when their lips touched I think Auran knew what had happened, I think we all felt the same thing at that moment when he raised his sword about his head.

My thoughts were for Raine, he would kill her before he would be sealed away, she buried herself in Hunter's chest, he pulled her tight and closed his eyes. I must admit, even though this is for historical purposes, I covered my eyes with my paws and could not watch. Louie told me that the blade only scratched her side, it was not a deep wound thank goodness. Auran was pulled back into the centre of Ethernia with the ruined castle of Vitam above him. I must admit too that, even though the ghosts were disappearing one by one, now finally free from Auran, I still feared the worst. Raine bled, it was not heavy but we all thought her to be in a dire condition, but as I said, we later found out she was fine. Hunter took his wife up in his arms and took her away from the castle, to the boat and back to the safety of his tree house. We all stayed behind to help with the clear up of the ghosts, some forgetting they were free, so we pointed them in the right direction while others decided to stay on Vitam.

Once the four elemental pixies, Talia and myself returned to the safety of Terrae we found Hunter below his tree house pacing like a sane man, he told us that Foog was tending to Raine. The other rulers of Ethernia wanted to know what had happened, Dallan was part of them. Talia gave them the news that Raine had done what she set out to do and sealed away Auran for good. She also addressed them in a very royal tone informing them of who Raine was. She proudly told them that she was the daughter of Terra, the niece of Jerrad and the rightful Queen of Terrae and a child of Life, the Queen of Vitam. For the records the King was informed, Dallan must have told him the news that not only was Auran defeated but the rightful ruler was Raine, there was proof by the seals she carried and used for the land. Let history know that the once King simply vanished from Terrae, no one knows where he went or when.

Days after being told the throne was left open, no one sat on the throne of Terrae. Talia came to my field and wished to see Raine, she at this time was recovering well after her encounter with Auran. I am not sure but I think the sealing ritual had taken some of her energy thus making it longer for the healing process to complete itself. Dallan was also with the young Princess, he had a royal scroll, he had been searching rooms that the King had kept locked, it seemed inside were royal documents stating that his ancestors had indeed cheated their way to the throne and when the rightful Heir returns then they ,must forfeit. He also found the scroll with Raine's birth, she called it a 'Birth Certificate' something they had in her world to confirm they were born and who they were. A needless thing in my eyes. It had her parents, her family line and of course, Auran and Jerrad. It seemed to be rather over whelming for her, she was a confirmed Firefly, she had a surname, her identity. Dallan did not seem to pick up on this and carried on that after the battle there was one more thing she needed to do for Ethernia, as she was the only child of Life within Ethernia, she must claim the throne of Vitam. Being the only Heir to that throne meant that she would finally reunite the four realms, making Ethernia complete.

At that point I felt it was right for everyone to leave Raine and Hunter alone, it was a lot of information for the newly Unioned couple to take in. I later returned with a meal for them, Raine asked me to stay, she asked if I knew her parents, I told her that there was no greater Queen than her mother Terra. I then decided to take her to their grave, Jerrad never once took Raine there, he said that it was not his place to tell Raine who she was, his sister forbid it. Should she ever return to Ethernia for any reason she should find out herself. Once we got there, to the royal sleeping place, Hunter and I left Raine alone with her parents.

Hunter confided in me, he was such a different man to the lost boy I knew, the crazy man who ran after Pompom's in the woods. He told me how Raine doubted herself, how everything was too much for her, he told me what he said to her. He said he would always stay by her side, providing he could go out and hunt Pompom's once in a while. I had tried to hide my laugher within, he asked if that was the right thing to say, it was, I felt proud of Hunter that day. He had truly grown into a man before my very eyes and I had almost been blind to it. He is of course still as mad as a fruit cake.

Once Raine had finished with her parents she had a different look about her, her eyes burned brightly with resolve as she told us she would do what was right, she would claim the throne of Vitam and do what she was born to do. But, she informed us there was something that needed to be done first.

We walked to the castle of Terrae where the many staff members were in disarray, Talia had gathered them in the throne room, trying to make some sense to the mess her brother had left behind.

As though it were the most natural thing in the world, Raine walked in, called for their attention and informed them of a great decision she had come to. She told them that she was the Heir to the throne of both Terrae and Vitam, that she was the niece of the last true King, but it was her wish that someone else rule Terrae in her place. She told them this person had the love and dedication a ruler needed, that the actions of this person were true to the land and the greater good. I did ponder at first if she was talking about me, I must document for history that I will never take the throne of any realm as my, longevity would cause complications. No, she turned to Talia and told her she wished her to rule in her place.

The history for Talia, ruler of Terrae was a great and glorious one. She took to the throne days after Raine named her ruler in her place. It took many lengths of paper work to complete this and Dallan was kept very busy. He told me that royal decrees such as this were very time consuming, so for any future reference let it be noted.

For a Queen to pass on rule to a person of non-royal blood a decree must be drawn up, should the ruler need guidance or advice then they must seek it from the blood Queen, they must also consult for any future acts of war.

Talia and Foog later married and ruled their realms united, traveling to and fro between A'ris and Terrae, they were indeed blessed with a family of six children. Under the new rulers law the land of Terrae returned to its beautiful state and all those who lost their homes were given new places of dwelling. I can say that I was suitably impressed with Talia's words, yet her actions were true and let history know that never was there a truer word spoken than those by Talia of Terrae.

For Vitam the healing process took longer than expected, although there were no citizens to heal, the land was almost dead. But after I inspected it closely, I discovered parts surrounding the ruined castle were alive. Using this earth I was able to create potions to revive the earth so new plants and vegetation could start anew. While I was brewing and studying, Raine and Hunter too to work, they wanted to clean up the remains of Vitam and build it anew. They were not alone in their toils. The rulers for the other realms sent help, they sent tools, food, plants, everything they needed to rebuild an entire realm.

Walt and his aquatic people ushered in the waters so the lakes and rivers that once ran through Vitam were once more alive with the harmonious sound of hushing. Of course once able to travel down the paths under the water, they were able to clean the beds and plant all sort of water based plants and flowers.

The Fire Chief, which I have come now to realise is his name, those of the land of Ignis have very little imagination for names. He came with his strongest people and they helped clear the land of rubble and ruin, they also helped in rebuilding the main vocal point of Vitam, the castle.

But the rulers of the other realms decided that it should be a palace, a great palace of white with marble staircases, trees of pink and white blossoms in the court yard and beautiful blossoms and all sorts of foliage for the grounds.

Talia and all of Terrae, including myself, began growing as many plants, trees and every kind of earth base thing you could think of for Vitam. Every day Hunter, Raine and I would travel to Vitam, work hard and return until we started again the next day.

Foog and his people decorated the palace and built many homes for the citizens who wanted to make Vitam their home, as well as the ghosts who decided to stay and not move on, they were give their own place to live their un-dead lives.

It took many months of work and love but when it was complete it was a sight to behold, Vitam was alive with a glowing light, brighter than it had ever been. The entire population of Ethernia came to the crowning of Raine and Hunter, she declared that everyone should be invited to Vitam where they held a grand party for all. And so, Raine and Hunter set up their home in their palace on Vitam, they attended the royal duties needed of them, the rulers decided it would be a good idea to meet every three quarters at the palace to discuss anything that needed to be done. Ethernia ran smoothly under the new care of Vitam, it was most excellent to see and still is.

As for Hunter and Raine, they were blessed with child, two in fact, a girl and a boy they lovingly named Terra and Jerrad. I thought this to be very fitting, Jerrad would have been so happy to know that his name lived on in some small way. They were helped by the four elemental Pixies who had raised Raine from a baby, Iris, Pearl, Maud and Louie stayed with them from the moment they moved to Vitam. I believe it was in their nature to mother and care and even though Raine was now a Queen, it never stopped them from mothering her still.

They raised their children well, often the other royal children would visit so the halls of the palace were never truly quiet, and that is why I never stayed there much, only to teach when they were older. It seemed that was my job from then on wards, to teach the children of Ethernia in the palace three times in a week. As the children got older, Raine and Hunter left the island of Vitam more to travel until the twins turned eighteen. Raine and Hunter decided it was time for them to leave the rulings of the country to their children, let history know that Raine herself said that royal life was nice, but a little too stuffy and boring, she wanted to travel and be free to do what she pleased.

I am pleased to say that once their children took the throne officially, they returned to the one place they liked to call home. The tree house in my field.

For all the years they had been away I had never once tore it down, I left it there, I even tended to it so once they returned, they could move in and live there as they did before they were King and Queen. Of course the spell around my house touched them, so their lives were slightly longer than most, they did age, but slowly. For they are human in creature where as I am not, so I live for a considerably longer period, I'm not sure how much longer though as I have been around for so many years. I still document the histories of Ethernia, hence this entry into my book, I think I shall write the entire history of when Raine came to

Ethernia, take her accounts of her life here and in her world and create a book dedicated to her. I think, if nothing else it would make for light reading and serve as a warning to future rulers of Vitam, never to release Auran.

Ethernia is still blossoming to this day, I often check that door Raine once used to travel between worlds, it would be a most curious thing if it were to open and another come through. Yet, the thought has passed me, what if someone were to go out, should the door be opened again, what of this other world Raine was sent to? What would happen, what could be on the other side I ask myself?

But I am just a cat, a smart, crazy cat I am told. I never understand myself at times, when others read my words they decree, 'oh, what a smart man this scholar must be, for his words are true and not muddled in any way.' Yet were they to meet me, they would say, 'oh what a crazy, mad wizard of a cat, a cat I say!' oh what a shock they would get. But I am just that, a cat named Cat, my family had no imagination you see, and forever shall I go on in my crazy way, living and writing the history of this world, this realm, this place we call Ethernia where a Firefly lives in my tree house and her children live on an island. For every time I see Raine I recalled how I, Cat of Terrae was there, when the lost Firefly came home.

ABOUT THE AUTHOR

Kayleigh Burdett lives on the edge of London with her partner and Son and is currently enjoying time off work to be a full time mother. She finds time whenever she can to write. At the moment, apart from writing parts to her 'Nightshade' series, she is also taking a personal challenge to write 12 novels in 12 months, starting in November 2013 and ending in November 2014. National Novel Writing Month starts and finishes the challenge. She is well on her way to getting to that half-way point.

This is Kayleigh Burdett's third Nanowrimo novel. She has been writing short stories and fan fiction since she was a child, but her first big novel came back in the early 00's when she took an idea and made it into her first 50k plus word novel.

Since 2003 she has been working hard on a series inspired from a dream, the 'Nightshade' series. The first has finally been complete and is in production, 'The Birth of Arcane' is the first really big novel and she is over joyed to finally share it with you.

CPSIA information can be obtained
at www.ICGtesting.com
Printed in the USA
BVOW03s1508070817
491384BV00001B/11/P